PRAISE FOR ANNE CHARNOCK

DREAMS BEFORE THE START OF TIME

WINNER OF THE 2018 ARTHUR C. CLARKE AWARD

SHORT-LISTED FOR THE 2017 BRITISH SCIENCE FICTION ASSOCIATION AWARD FOR BEST NOVEL

"Arthur C Clarke award goes to 'classic' novel exploring the limits of pregnancy . . . focuses on changing reproductive science, hailed as 'rich but unshowy.'"

—*Guardian*

"*Dreams Before the Start of Time* is a slow burn, but its darkness is lowkey, an undercurrent of disquiet that never overspills. The fascist dystopia creeps in on little cat feet, never announcing itself with guns and explosions. It is not even resisted; it simply *wins*."

—Vajra Chandrasekera, *Strange Horizons*

"Deceptively intimate, this is big-idea SF reminiscent of the societal changes mapped across generational sagas like *Foundation* or the Mars trilogy."

—Alasdair Stuart, *Locus Magazine*

"Highly enjoyable and thought-provoking . . . The willingness to experiment with viewpoint through time, as well as present a human agenda (what little science fiction these days can say that), make the novel very worthwhile. The futuristic technology depicted is extremely likely—in development as we speak—making the novel groundbreaking."

—Jesse Hudson, *Speculiction*

"I'm delighted and inspired by Anne Charnock's writing talent, her contemplative, forensic, insatiably curious approach to speculative fiction. The three novels she has produced to date constitute a significant literary achievement."

—Nina Allan, author of *The Rift*, winner of the 2018
Kitschies Red Tentacle Award

"Anne Charnock's characters are completely recognisable . . . [her] writing is calm and quiet . . . unusual and thought provoking."

—Gwenda Major, *NB* magazine

"Charnock's interest is always in the human aspect first: her characters are real, living, breathing individuals; lost in some ways, directive in others. Anne Charnock is now solidified as one of my favorite SF authors."

—*From Couch to Moon*

SLEEPING EMBERS OF AN ORDINARY MIND

INCLUDED IN THE *GUARDIAN'S* BEST SCIENCE FICTION AND FANTASY BOOKS OF 2015

"Anne Charnock's *Sleeping Embers of an Ordinary Mind* is an expert braiding together of past, present, and future that puts a fifteenth-century Italian female artist centre stage to say penetrating things about womanhood, creativity, and history."

—Adam Roberts, *Guardian*

"*Sleeping Embers of an Ordinary Mind* is certainly one of 2015's tip-top releases in science fiction."

—Jesse Hudson, *Speculiction*

"This quiet, lovely, and exquisitely crafted novel is itself a masterclass in composition . . . As in her debut novel, *A Calculated Life*, the clarity and refined elegance of Charnock's prose is a significant achievement."

—Nina Allan, author of *The Rift*, winner of the 2018 Kitschies Red Tentacle Award

"The feminist elements of *Sleeping Embers of the Ordinary Mind* are elusively contradictory, so much like life!, making this one of those thinking books— the kind with embers smoldering until a second visit. I look forward to more from Anne Charnock."

—*From Couch to Moon*

"The centuries-spanning story gives the mystery an epic feel."

—*Kirkus Reviews*

A CALCULATED LIFE

SHORT-LISTED FOR THE 2013 PHILIP K. DICK AND KITSCHIES GOLDEN TENTACLE AWARDS

"[*A Calculated Life*] is lovingly crafted, beautifully made in the economical, expert way a piece of Arts and Crafts furniture is made—pure lines, and perfectly suited to its intended purpose . . . Anne Charnock is clearly a gifted and sensitive author of acute intelligence, writing science fiction of a kind— quiet, intense, thoughtful—we could do with more of."

—Nina Allan, author of *The Rift*, winner of the 2018 Kitschies Red Tentacle Award

"Charnock is a subtle worldbuilder . . . For readers who want a smart, subtle exploration of human emotion and intelligence, this is an excellent choice."

—Alix E. Harrow, *Strange Horizons*

"A very noteworthy book . . . What [Charnock] shares with [Philip K.] Dick is the ability to write unease . . . She has fascinating, complex things to say about work, sex, family and hope."

—Adam Roberts, author of *Jack Glass*, winner of the 2012 BSFA Best Novel Award

"This story puts us inside one of the most interesting perspectives I've encountered in recent fiction. Jayna's perspective is so unique that I would happily have followed her anywhere, and, as a consequence, the cleverness of this plot almost snuck up on me. A smart, stylish, emotionally compelling book with literary richness and sci-fi smarts."

—Susan DeFreitas, author of *Hot Season*

"Charnock [is] an astute observer herself, [and] what results is an inquiry into feminism and society that will make the reader truly pause to compare their own experiences and perceptions."

—Jesse Hudson, *Speculiction*

BRIDGE
108

BRIDGE 108

ANNE CHARNOCK

47N⬥RTH

Text copyright © 2020 by Anne Charnock
All rights reserved.

Published by 47North, Seattle
www.apub.com

Amazon, the Amazon logo, and 47North are trademarks of Amazon.com, Inc., or its affiliates.

ISBN-13: 9781542006071 (hardcover)
ISBN-10: 1542006074 (hardcover)

ISBN-13: 9781542006088 (paperback)
ISBN-10: 1542006082 (paperback)

Cover design by David Drummond

Printed in the United States of America

First edition

For my family

Contents

PART 1

CHAPTER 1

CALEB

At the rooftop sink, with the sun already burning my back, I turn on the cold tap, lean over and rinse my itchy scalp and scarecrow hair. Cold water never runs from the cold tap—not since summer started, not even in the morning after the storage tank has cooled during the night. The tank bakes all day in the sunshine, and by the evening the cold tap always runs hot.

Just because the tap is labelled *C* doesn't mean it is *C*.

Ma Lexie calls out: "Caleb, over here. Now."

She leads me across the flat roof of our housing block, past the solar arrays, towards a wooden hut—the living quarters of Mr. Ben, the overseer. I walk as close as I can behind her because she smells like fresh oranges. She looks as light as a feather. She could float away in the breeze. Her thin, sleeveless dress is printed with wild flowers and owls. As the fabric ripples, the owls with stretched-out wings seem to fly. I'm wearing only my shorts, and I'm barefoot. My hair drips onto my shoulders and down my back, bringing a memory of being tickled.

Ma Lexie swipes the air above her head with her right hand. Is she waving to Odette? I glance across at the roof of the next housing block. No, she can't be. Odette is facing away from us, reaching up with both hands. Squinting, I see she's cutting dead flowers from a climbing rose. I worry about the thorns. Don't prick yourself, Odette.

Ma Lexie is swiping back and forth as though smacking a tall person across the face, first with the back of her hand and then her open palm.

"Don't panic, Ma Lexie," I say. An early-rising honeybee is harassing her. But I reckon the bee is still sleepy, like me.

We're on the bees' flight path from the hives, two roofs away, to the lavender farms west of the enclave. When I first arrived here five months ago, Ma Lexie told me I'd get used to the bees. They'd continue on their way if I didn't make a fuss. She's making a fuss herself and mutters the usual complaints: "Shouldn't be allowed," and then, "Affecting my business."

"The enclave council should ban the hives, Ma Lexie, shouldn't they?" I'm trying to nudge her towards a better mood because I reckon I'm heading straight for trouble. In her left hand she grips the candy-striped shirt that I worked on yesterday. Mr. Ben was disgusted with how I'd sewn the shirt's collar. He yanked my ear, hard. Called me an idiot and told me to stop work on the shirt. He shouted, said he'd shift me back to baby work—unpicking seams, sewing on buttons—if I couldn't think of anything sensible to make. I guess he complained to the boss, Ma Lexie, about me.

Anyway, what does *he* know? After the yanking, he walked off, and I watched his massive, round back as he grumped away across the roof to his hut. I snuck to the back of our work shed and pushed the shirt under my sleeping roll. I'd already unpicked the collar, and in its place I'd started sewing a strip of dark mock fur. It made the shirt look mean, dangerous. A brilliant remake, and I thought Ma Lexie would agree. I carried on with the half-finished job during our evening playtime. Zach and Mikey wanted me to join the button-flicking game that I'd invented, but I told them to practise without me.

Ma Lexie grips my shoulder as we stand outside Mr. Ben's hut. She shakes the shirt at me. I feel hurt; Ma Lexie had dug around in my things while I was washing at the sink.

She says, "Mr. Ben came to see me yesterday. Not happy about your work, told me about this!"

I jump in fast. "Mr. Ben knows shit. I'm finishing the shirt in my own time, Ma Lexie. It's going to look brilliant when it's nicely pressed." I'd planned to finish sewing the fur collar and sneak it into the pile for pressing. Honest, I thought Ma Lexie would like it. I thought she'd smile.

"Mr. Ben wants me to throw you out. Send you to work at the family premises."

I stare at her. We're both wide-eyed. The family premises, as she calls it, is the centre of the family's rubbish and recycling business. I've never been there. I've been off the roof for less than twenty minutes a week.

She throws the hut's door wide open and steps inside. I grab it as it swings back and keep it steady in the warm breeze.

"This is yours now, Caleb."

I step inside for the first time. It stinks of Mr. Ben. Sweat and chlorine. My empty stomach tightens.

"Where . . . ?" I look around, expecting him to leap out and clout me one.

"I've decided Mr. Ben isn't cut out for the fashion business. No imagination."

"But where . . . ?"

"He's better suited to the dirty side of the operation, don't you think?" She frowns at me. "You won't be seeing him anytime soon. So, clean this place out. Look after it better than he did. You're the overseer now."

I look down at the shirt, and she hands it over.

"Any of this fur left?" she asks. I nod. "Then, make as many as you can. I think they'll sell."

She's totally right. "I need better quality shirts than this, Ma Lexie. I want them to look . . . *sharp*. Tailored office shirts, that sort of thing. They'll look like a uniform for a team or a gang."

She raises an eyebrow, hesitating. Does she think I'm being dumb?

She says, "Finish this one today, and I'll try it out tomorrow at the market stall. And from now on, you'll be doing the weekend markets with me."

The markets. I want to hug her, but I've never seen anyone touch Ma Lexie. It's like she's too perfect, like the touch would burn. And I don't know why we call her Ma. She only looks about thirty. I kneel down and kiss the hem of her dress.

"Up," she says.

"The shirt will be amazing, Ma Lexie."

She digs into a pocket in her dress and holds out two keys on a greasy black ribbon, which I've only ever seen hanging around Mr. Ben's neck, the keys nestled in his thick mat of chest hair. One key is for the padlock for Mr. Ben's hut. *My* hut. The other is for the steel door—the roof access to the building's internal stairs.

"Your new job starts in five minutes," she says. "Come down to my flat and collect the kids' breakfasts."

As I reach out for the keys, she pulls back and I freeze. It's a hoax. She'll laugh, and Mr. Ben will leap out and whack me. She says, slowly and gently, "No second chance, Caleb. Don't let me catch you going downstairs and wandering off. You know I'd find you. Everyone knows Ma Lexie." I take the keys. Before she releases her grip, she says, "When everyone sees you at the market with me, they will know exactly who you are. That you're my new boy. Everyone will memorise your face. Understand?" And with that she heads back across the roof and retreats down the stairs to her top-floor flat. Yes, I can trust her—what you see is what you get with Ma Lexie.

I'm Ma Lexie's new boy. I like the sound of that. Better than "the kid dumped by the road." It's a new start.

I can't do much in five minutes to clear Mr. Ben's mess, but I drag out the mattress and prop it against the side of the hut. If the mattress soaks up the sun, it's likely to "air out," as my mother would say. I've no idea what "airing out" means. Does a smell dry out? Won't the bedbugs thrive in the heat? Or does bright light kill them off? Anyway, until I'm rid of the stench, I'll continue to sleep with the sky as my blanket.

I jam Mr. Ben's wooden chair—*my* wooden chair—against the door to keep it open. I step inside and place my hand against the side wall, then smell my palm. Mr. Ben's sweating, farting, belching sticks in the timber grain. Sure of it. I wonder if Ma Lexie will give me some paint if I ask nicely; a coat of paint will seal him in for good.

Empty bottles, old clothes, worn-down sandals. Why didn't he throw them away? What a pig. And the stink—I hold my hand to my face, breathe through my mouth. Has something died in here? A mouse? A whole nest of dead mice? I check the hut's roof. Will it leak when it rains? Across the far end of the hut, there's a shelf with hooks screwed to the underside. I'll use them to hang up my clothes. I pick up a padlock from the floor, check which key will open it. I'll have no worries about my stuff going missing, about anyone poking around in my backpack.

I told Ma Lexie my documents were lost, but I still have them. Mother sewed them into the straps of my backpack. She made me sleep with my pack strapped with a belt to my arm, while she slept across the tent's entrance.

As soon as this place is clean, I'll unpack my winter clothes—could be too raggy to keep—my chess set, my comics. But still, I'm not sure the hut is a great idea. It's not just the smell I'm worried about. It's going to feel strange being on my own again, when the door's closed. There's no window. Should I tell Ma Lexie I don't want it? It reminds me too much of the tent.

In one way, I felt safe in the windowless tent. Anyone sneaking around the camp at night couldn't see me—see that I slept alone. But then, I couldn't see out. I spent hours wide awake—imagining people plotting on the other side of the tent's red fabric. I lay there scared out of my head by each and every tiny noise. And that colour! Every morning, opening my eyes to a red world. Blue would have been better—the colour of the sky.

I back out of the hut, walk across to the edge of our flat roof. I grip the railing that runs the length of the knee-high parapet, and I gaze westward beyond the grey enclave, across the English border, to the distant mountains of Wales. I feel proud of myself for getting this far. My parents, wherever they are, would be especially proud of me today with my sudden promotion.

The birds will tell them. I wipe my eyes and glance back across my shoulder—no one's looking. My mother started all her tall tales the same way: "You know, Caleb, a sparrow came to my windowsill today, and she told me a strange tale . . ." A chiffchaff sometimes visited her windowsill, or a lark. As I grew older, I'd roll my eyes at her when she started like this. But I still played along.

Mother had such plans for me, but I'm making my own future now—and it's nothing like her dream. She had our lives mapped out. Every night, along our journey through the Pyrenees, through France, we lay in the tent, and she described a new home, somewhere not too hot, not too dry. As if preparing me for disappointment, she whispered that our new home might be smaller than the one we left behind in Spain. First, she said, we would "introduce ourselves" at a reception centre—a doctor would check my health and repeat the childhood inoculations I'd had against common diseases. More important, she told me I'd have another forced inoculation, a special one. Better late than never, she said. I shouldn't complain if I felt sick for a few days because this extra inoculation, she said over and over, was the best indication that a country was worth reaching. In England, all children had this special inoculation at birth, with booster injections spread over time, a system that freed everyone from ever forming addictions—people were less violent, no compulsive gambling, no drug crime. Much safer.

"They don't need troublemakers, Caleb," she'd say. I tried to tell her that I wasn't a troublemaker, but she'd shush me. When Mother disappeared, I had to make my own decisions.

I've been lucky. Skylark found me on the road in northern France, not far from the coast. She arrived pedalling an electric bicycle with a sidecar. She wore a leather jacket with a collar of long feathers—black feathers with shining glints of green. At that point, I'd joined a new group, and we were resting for a day. Skylark hung out with us all, let the children stroke her feathered collar.

I had a good feeling as soon as she told me her name. I could pass as her kid brother; she didn't look much older than twenty. She was shocked I had no parent with me, said she'd take me under her wing. She laughed. It was a joke, she said—Skylark's wing. I impressed her with how I'd managed on my own. When I explained I was heading with the others to a reception centre, she said *that* was the worst possible plan.

I have to admit, I didn't like the idea of those inoculations. Skylark told me: "Late inoculation? Bad idea. You're as sick as a dog for weeks. It's best having the first injection at birth, when the side effects are negligible. And, you know, Caleb, you won't be the same afterwards." I remember she snapped her fingers twice in front of my face and said, "You'll lose your spark." I asked if she'd lost *her* spark, and she laughed. Said she'd been on the road a long time, skipped her adult booster.

And those reception centres, she warned me, keep you for months before handing you over to a work camp outside one of the enclaves, and there were no proper schools on the camps as Mother thought. See, Mother had it all wrong. Skylark said I'd be a slave for years, indentured at the camp, doing filthy work on the fish farms and at the incinerators—and there's no guarantee of getting the right to stay.

Skylark offered to help me but warned me not to tell the other people in my group because she couldn't help everyone. She had space in her sidecar for just one, and she thought I had—what did she say?—*real grit.*

She chose *me.* But the journey with Skylark was worse than I expected, and—if I'm telling the whole truth—once or twice I wondered if she'd tricked me. It was confusing; I thought Skylark wanted to rescue only me, but there were others, and we met up with them near the coast. She'd rescued all of them, one at a time, and I was the last to arrive. Once we'd crossed the Channel—the worst part, which I don't like to think about—everything happened so fast. Skylark dropped me off with Ma Lexie, and I haven't been hungry or cold since then.

I turn my back to the parapet railing and look over at the work shed. The kids aren't up yet. They'll be happy about my promotion, but I can't allow any slacking. I always tell them: the sooner they finish their work, the sooner they can play. But with Mr. Ben gone, they won't be afraid any more. Ma Lexie should find some older boys, like me, if she wants to make the business successful. Zach and Mikey are young for this work. They need too much help. And I know she never takes girls. Skylark told me so.

When Father finds me, or when I find him, he'll be impressed. I'm only twelve years old and I'm in charge.

I'm not sure how Father will track me down. Five weeks after he left, his messages stopped. Maybe he fell ill and he's in a hospital somewhere. At least we have a fail-safe. I'm sure he'll eventually return home, and I imagine the scene every night before I fall asleep. He'll open the tin—slotted into the stone wall surrounding the graveyard—and read Mother's message. I watched her write it: *We can't wait here any longer. If you've sent messages to us during the past twelve weeks, we haven't received them. We'll follow you to England—we'll be fine with Caleb's English. They won't turn us away if we accept indentured work. Then we'll find our compatriots in Manchester. We know you are safe. We feel it in our hearts.*

When I think of compatriots, I think of old people with white hair, sitting around with nothing to do. Drinking tea and complaining. I think I'm better off with Ma Lexie and the other kids. Ma Lexie says she's putting aside a little money each week for me, and when I'm fifteen she'll hand it over.

One day, definitely, I will find my family's compatriots. I'll have to tell them about Mother, about how tired she felt, and how she became confused and started sleepwalking. She disappeared one night. The people we were travelling with couldn't wait for her to return, but I refused to leave. I searched for days and days, looking in the hedgerows and ditches, but nothing. She didn't find her way back, and, in the end, I had no choice. I sorted through her stuff and decided what to take with me. I traded her clothes. I unpicked the straps of her backpack, removed her documents and the last of our money. She told me at the start of our journey that money had only two uses until we reached Father—to buy food and to pay bribes. So, I took the money, a page from her passport, her sewing kit, and a photograph of my father, which would help me to trace him.

After three weeks without Mother, living and sleeping alone in my tent, I decided to join a small group of migrants who came through, heading north "towards kinder weather." They kept saying the gods were angry. My parents never talked about the gods, but I didn't say so.

Skylark's eyes lit up when I said I used to help my mother with her sewing. She messed up my hair, laughed and said, "I've just the job for you."

I smile to myself because she was right. This job is perfect. It's hard work, but I don't miss school any more, only my friends. Yesterday, though, I nearly lost my nerve—pushing the needle through fur—it woke up memories, and the soles of my feet began to sweat.

———

I wash the keys, and in front of the two kids, I hang the keys around my neck. They grin, and Zach says, "I heard him leave last night. Gone for good?" Mikey offers a high-five, but I ignore him.

"Hurry. I'll bring breakfast. I want you both washed and dressed double quick."

As I slot the key into the stairwell door, I say to myself that the worst is over. Yesterday, I was one of the kids. Today, I'm Ma Lexie's right-hand man. I pull open the door, lock it behind me and walk down the concrete steps.

There's another voice besides Ma Lexie's inside the flat. I place my ear to the door. A man's voice. The same man as before?

When I first arrived at this housing block, hand in hand with Skylark, I stayed in Ma Lexie's flat. Never went out for three full weeks. Ma Lexie said I deserved a good rest, and I must eat three meals every day. She brought home a kitten for me to play with. And a man came to check my teeth. Another time, Ma Lexie came home with a woman—a nurse or a doctor—who told me to undress, down to my underpants. She checked me over and asked about the scar on my thigh. I told her it happened a long time ago, but I think she knew I was lying. I didn't want to talk about it.

Ma Lexie positioned my mattress in the kitchen. I couldn't see her bed from where I lay. She gave me earplugs so—as she said—she could have privacy. I knew what she meant because, on the road, I'd hear grunting and yelpy sounds from other tents in the night. Those noises didn't bother me. But the earplugs did—dirty with old earwax. I used them all the same—scratched off the worst. After all, Skylark and Ma Lexie had saved me.

I knock and the boyfriend opens the door. He smiles and says, "Hello, mate. Long time no see."

Ma Lexie passes me the breakfast box and a flask. I try to look past her into the flat.

"Is the kitten here?" I ask. The boyfriend smirks, making me feel embarrassed. I'm the overseer and I shouldn't be asking about kittens. I say, standing to attention, "Thank you, Ma Lexie. I won't let you down. I'll do a better job than Mr. Ben."

The door closes and I hear the boyfriend laugh. I look down the stairs. I've never been in the stairwell alone. On Sundays, Mr. Ben took us down to the street, handed out pocket money and took us to a neighbouring block, to some relative of Ma Lexie's, an old man. He sold sweets and second-hand toys from the living room of his flat. One time, I persuaded Zach and Mikey to pool their money with mine, and we bought a pack of playing cards. It was worth it because the kids were getting so bored, and I was tired of inventing games. But they found it tough waiting an extra week for sweets.

I climb back up the stairs. One day, I'll have my own flat. I'll look out for my neighbours, make myself useful, and I'll win the janitor's job, like Ma Lexie. That's the easiest way I can see to make serious money, because only a janitor can run a business on an enclave roof. All I'd have to do in return is brush and mop the stairwell and wash down the solar arrays. I've already decided that I'll run a petting zoo on my rooftop or, even better, an aviary with cockatiels, budgies and lovebirds—a business I can run without any help. On the roofs surrounding Ma Lexie's, there's a laundry, a strawberry farm and my favourite—where Odette works—a garden with trellises, climbing flowers and birdbaths. Truth is, the birdbaths are in my imagination because I like to remind myself of the one in our small garden at home. I haven't visited Odette's roof, but when Ma Lexie's in a good mood, I hope I'll persuade her to take me there. I guess she might be frightened because beyond the rooftop garden, on the next block, stand the wretched beehives.

———

Zach and Mikey watch me closely. The skin under Zach's right eye starts to twitch, and he lifts a finger to press down on his eye socket. He's worried, I guess, that I'll pick on him like Mr. Ben did. We sit outside the work shed on a raffia mat—a picnic, enclave style. I set out the flatbreads, the bruised apples, and I start pouring juice in our chipped beakers.

It's unfair to make the boys feel anxious, so I half fill my beaker and fill each of theirs to the top.

"It's market day tomorrow, boys." They nod at me. "We need to finish all the clothes on the table. Any problems—come to me. Let's not disappoint Ma Lexie. Hey?" They nod again. "Start on the easy jobs and make sure you finish them neatly. Push anything difficult to one side—I'll take a look at them this afternoon. I've a special order to finish this morning for Ma Lexie. And don't forget to wash your hands after breakfast. Okay?"

"Mr. Ben is gone for good?" asks Mikey.

"Yes. But we mustn't mess up. Or I'll be following Mr. Ben, and you two will be back on the street."

I take my drink and flatbread and pace the rooftop boundary. It's all the exercise I get. I lean over to check the street. Four floors below me, people are rushing to the shuttle station—off to Manchester, the city our enclave serves. I tried to tell Mother that I didn't want an office job, but she didn't listen. I wanted to work outdoors. After watching Ma Lexie, I've decided I want a life in business. I could be Ma Lexie's business partner. When she's old, I'll run the whole operation for her—choose the recycled textiles for our remake clothes, expand the team and build a fashion brand.

My plan is much better than Mother's. According to Mother, once we earned our right to stay, we'd take a flat in one of the enclaves, which are cheap because everything is subsidised, she said, for people who agree to live there. And then we'd find Father. When I turn eighteen, Mother said I could apply for an implant, cognitive chipping, and there'd be no looking back then. But how's that going to happen now, with two missing parents? I'll never gain approval for an implant—my family might be criminals, or politicos, for all that the authorities know.

Mother dreamed of a life one day in the city suburbs. She'd retire with Father and I'd support them. I'd be married in this dream, and my wife and I would be city workers. We'd all live together. But that was Mother's dream, and I think her ideas were old-fashioned.

———

We work late every Friday, and today we're even later than normal. We've pressed all the finished clothes, folded them neatly into plastic containers, which are stacked, ready for the market. Ma Lexie bangs on the steel door, and I jump up to unlock it for her. She's carrying a deep bowl with our fish-and-rice supper. This one day of the week, Ma Lexie sits at the worktable and eats with us. She serves. In silence—for we are much too tired to talk—we begin wolfing down our meal. I glance around the table because, sitting quietly together like this, I imagine we look like a family.

Ma Lexie pushes away her empty dish. I stand up and start to clear the table, but she shouts, "Zach! You move the dishes. It's your job now."

I blurt out: "Let me do it one last time, Ma Lexie. Look how tired he is. He worked so hard today, believe me."

She stands up, folds her arms and glowers at the younger boy. "Do as I say, Zach." She leaves, and Zach takes our dishes to the rooftop sink to rinse them.

I collect my sleeping roll from the back of the work shed, push it under one arm and heave my backpack on my shoulder. Dog tired, I drag a sweeping brush behind me as I step past the solar arrays towards the overseer's hut, determined to sweep out the worst of Mr. Ben's junk.

I'll push his junk into a pile, cover it with one of our tarps. Then I'll feel happy to move my stuff in tonight.

First, I dare myself to check the mattress. I stoop down, not too close, and breathe in. It's okay at the edge. I stretch across to the middle of the mattress. Still smells bad. I won't sleep on it tonight. I turn the mattress over so the other side will bake in the sun tomorrow. It might be okay by night-time.

As I straighten up, a plastic bottle clatters across the roof a metre behind me. Nice shot! I look across, wave to Odette, and she waves back. She likes to send a message at this time of day. Almost a routine. I glanced across at her during the day as she served drinks to the garden's visitors. They pay a membership and expect good service. And there's such a long waiting list for membership, that visits by each person can only add up to one hour a week. Odette keeps a record, and she's told me that everything in the garden has to be perfect every minute of the day—it's stressful.

I wish I could meet Odette face-to-face.

It isn't easy having a long-distance friend but we manage. We call across with one-word greetings. Mainly we throw messages in this short plastic bottle. We've put a stone inside; the extra weight helps. Before we settled on this particular container and this size of stone, we lost a few messages when they fell short, ended up in the street. It took us a while to perfect our messaging. In those days, while we practised, we'd wait until the street was quiet before making an attempt. Odette has the real knack. Her throws are more accurate than mine. I like that about her.

I drag out Mr. Ben's chair, sit down facing Odette's roof and pop open the bottle's lid. I peer in—I'm being careful because last week I found a live beetle under her crumpled message. She won't catch me again. And I'm planning my revenge. I pull out the paper and flatten it against my thigh. Her written English isn't good: *Wats goin on your roof. I seen no fat man tday.* I reach over and grab a pen from the side pocket of my backpack. I correct her spelling when I reply: *What is going . . . I saw . . . today.* Then I write: *Mister Ben is history. He's gone for good. I am the new overseer.* She might not know the word "overseer," so I add: *I'm the new Mister Ben. Going to market tomorrow with Ma Lexie.* The label on the bottle—a smiling peanut—makes me laugh as I fasten the lid.

I take three strides backwards, imagine the flight path, run forward three steps and launch the bottle. Too far to the left, too high, it bounces on the parapet railing and drops onto the roof. Odette has her hands on her head. I hold out my hands. *No sweat.*

How old is Odette? I haven't ever asked, and she doesn't know my age either. Anyway, what does it matter? We don't have a street of friends to choose from. I haven't noticed anyone my age on any other neighbouring building. There's the old man who hangs out laundry, and the old woman who farms the strawberries. At a guess, I think Odette's older than me, fourteen or even fifteen. When she finishes reading my note, she looks up and shouts, "Well. Done." She scribbles a note again and whirls around, readies herself and makes a short run up. She throws the bottle and I catch it. What a thrower!

The message reads: *Clever boy. Bring me a prez from the markit.* There's no space left for a reply, and I'm too tired to go hunting for another piece of paper. I wave, give the thumbs-up and wave again.

Opening up my backpack, I dig out a roll of papers and add Odette's latest message to the top. It feels good to collect them together, as if I'm telling myself I can still make friends, given the chance. Flipping through them, I notice we never talk about the past. What's the point, and what can you write on the edge of some packaging material? If I had a whole sheet of paper I might tell her more. I'd like to tell her that my parents are educated—my father is an English teacher, and my mother a city clerk. In her spare time, she sewed costumes for the local amateur theatre group. My mother once complained that people assumed all the road walkers were poor, that we all left our homes because we had nothing to lose. I wouldn't tell Odette that my father was strict, and my mother didn't really listen to me.

I sweep out the hut, throw my rucksack inside and fasten the padlock on the outside of the door. My sleeping roll fits between the solar arrays—they'll offer a shield if the wind gets up during the night. Lying down, I feel peaceful for the first time today. The scar on my thigh starts to itch. I rub my finger along the lumpy line. It feels oddly soft.

——

After the first attack, Mother told me: "Those wicked people, they don't know anything about us. They attack the fear that lives deep inside, rotting them." In the middle of the night, they had rampaged through our camp, slitting open many of the tents. Mother and I woke when we heard screams, and we ran off. The young men and women in our group—those without children to defend—they ran at our attackers and fought in the mud. Afterwards, when we came out of hiding, we found that many of our companions were injured, and we did our best to help them.

The injuries were bad. Our camp cook was bleeding from a deep wound on his upper arm. Someone had stopped the blood flow with a belt fastened tight above the cut. But the wound needed stitching, and we had no medic. At the start of the journey we had a midwife, but she left us for another group heading east.

My mother took control. She lit a fire and boiled water because, she said, everyone knows that's the first job in an emergency. She took out her sewing kit and held a needle in the hottest part of the flame. "The middle of the flame isn't the right place," she told me. "If you put the needle there, it will come out covered in soot." I couldn't believe my eyes. My mother, totally focused, so brave.

She said, "Find some spirits, Caleb. Vodka. Someone will have a bottle."

And that's when I started my first ever job—doctor's assistant. I watched her pour vodka over the wound, scissors and needle. She boiled the black thread. She examined the cook's torn flesh as I'd seen her in the past examining a ripped dress. She took her scissors and trimmed the ragged edges of his skin, saying, "Don't look away, Caleb. You should learn how to do this. Look here! I need a neat edge so I can close the wound properly."

Mother's sewing kit lies at the bottom of my backpack in a biscuit tin. A tin of chocolate fingers.

Mother became important in our group after that night. She began making rules. The young children had *not* to wander around barefoot when we camped. Otherwise, they had stupid accidents. When we made camp each night, she told everyone where to pile our waste, so that sharp tins and bottles were out of harm's way.

The second attack came in daylight. We'd walked for days on quiet country roads surrounded by gentle rolling fields, which were muddied by early spring rainstorms. We could see for miles because the fields had no hedges. And we slept in small woods where we felt safer. We always cleared up after ourselves; we didn't want to annoy the farmers. But we couldn't avoid walking through one village, and looking back, we should have expected trouble. We rested in the village square while we took turns to fill our water bottles from a small fountain. No one shouted at us, but they all stared. Four men—looked like builders, muscular and tanned, one with paint splatters on his forearms—they stood close, legs wide apart, arms folded. Scowling.

We left as soon as we could. On the outskirts, a small van pulled up in front of us. Someone threw out a bin bag and sped off. My mother's friend poked the bag, looked inside and found a pile of stale bread and pastries, probably intended for a pigsty. But I thought it was kind, like someone cared. We shared them out.

A second parting gift came an hour later at a crossroads. A farm building hid our attackers from view. Seven of them came out holding knives, and I recognised the guy with paint splatters. Housepainter turned hard man. His arms weren't folded now—he held an old shotgun, the barrel hinged open. Snapped it shut and shot above our heads. We scattered. I ran off the road, pulling Mother across the muddy field. They ran through us, pushed Mother to the ground. When they ran off, I saw my leg was bleeding.

I sometimes think that if I hadn't been injured, I'd still be with Mother. She couldn't handle it. She cleaned mud out of my wound and stitched it—twelve stitches in all—her hand trembling. She didn't *say* anything, but under the surface I think she freaked out. Me, being injured, losing blood. The skin didn't even need trimming, but the stitches were the worst ever. Other injured people needed help, but I saw she was struggling to keep a grip. We swapped jobs. I took the needle from her hand. *She* poured salty water on the wound—she'd learned that salty water worked better than vodka—and held the needle in the flame, while *I* stitched the wounds.

I made a bad job of the first one. Mother mumbled, as though she didn't care, that I'd trimmed too much skin away. We moved on to a man with a nasty slash across his back. He was hairy and the light was poor. I found it difficult to see exactly what I was doing as I pushed the needle through his skin, through his hair.

I couldn't help thinking of him yesterday when I stitched the fur collar—when I pushed my needle through the pelt.

———

A scream rips me from my sleep. I hear another scream. It's a catfight. I open my eyes but I haven't escaped my dream. In a ploughed field, I struggle to pin my tent across the furrows as someone shouts, "Wolves."

It's true; we often heard animal cries at night. But they weren't wolves.

I wish I could sleep better. I wake two or three times most nights, and each time I fall back asleep the dreams become stranger and stranger. I fight in my sleep now and then, and wake to find myself hitting out, sometimes bruising myself on the metal stands of the solar arrays.

I don't really mind dreaming about the journey because I hope to see Mother as she used to be, before she became untidy and quiet. I roll onto my back, look up at the stars, and I hear her soft, clear voice from a time when everything was normal, when Father still lived with us: "Have you finished your homework, Caleb?" And then her voice is gone. I push myself up on one elbow, force my mind to clear.

I imagine the day to come—leaving the roof, walking through the enclave with Ma Lexie. I remember when I arrived here in darkness with Skylark, my surprise at seeing streets with no trees. It felt like a prison town without a perimeter wall. Blocks of flats, all the same size, separated by narrow streets and side alleys. Where I came from, every street was lined with trees, though many were dying back—bare branches poking out from the greenery, reaching for help.

Skylark led me up the stairs to Ma Lexie's flat and knocked. Ma Lexie let us in, and, without being asked, Skylark filled the kitchen sink with hot water. She drew a curtain across the kitchen area, gave me a cloth and told me to strip off. "Time to clean up," she said. I must have stunk. I hadn't washed in hot water in weeks. I peeled off my sweater and two T-shirts, and Skylark—without coming around the curtain—handed me some clothes in a pile. I placed them on the floor away from the sink and smoothed my hand over the fresh, clean cloth.

Above the sound of splashing water, I caught a few snatches of conversation—some talk about money, and I heard Skylark say, ". . . tall for his age." Ma Lexie asked, "Is he inoculated?" I didn't hear Skylark's reply, but Ma Lexie said, "Good. That's how I like them."

———

Before setting off to school, back home, I'd look down from our balcony, peer through the trees, to see if my friends were playing in the street. Often my friend Leo shouted from below: "Come down, come down, Caleb. We need you." It felt good to hear that. But my parents didn't like me to play football before school. Instead, my father would test me on the vocabulary lists he'd given me the night before.

Father walked me to school every day on his way to work. He would quiz me about my schoolwork because he wanted to get my brain started. He said I was too slow in the morning. I didn't like to tell him that I wasn't interested in many of my lessons. He wanted me to do well, but I knew I couldn't be like him. He once said, "You'll need to look after your mother and me one day. Our pensions will cover only the basics. It's your responsibility." I didn't understand him because I thought we were better off than most families. It was the first time he talked to me about money in a serious way. I wish I'd asked Mother on our long journey: *Were we poor?* And, looking back, I think I was so used to walking with Father to school that it felt strange to find myself walking every morning, as a migrant, with Mother. I never got used to that.

I roll up my bedding, stand and stretch out my arms. If Ma Lexie sells my fur-collared shirt today, I'll be the apple of her eye. Maybe I was meant for this kind of life. Working with my hands, helping Ma Lexie in the market. I can't wait.

Suddenly, I jump out of my skin—a clattering. I swivel around and see a new message bottle by the hut's door. Why's Odette messaging so early? I pick up the bottle and look around, but I can't see her. I pull out an empty packet of marigold seeds. The sides are slit open, and inside there's a message: *In the markit, find me a small torch. Throw it to me tonite. Do not miss.*

CHAPTER 2

MA LEXIE

I t's too damned quiet up there on the roof. Mr. Ben would be barging around by now, knocking stuff over, scraping back chairs. I look up at the ceiling. Come on, Caleb. Don't fall at the first hurdle, for God's sake. You need to prove yourself today.

I suppose he tossed and turned last night, overexcited about helping on the stall. But I shouldn't make excuses for him. He's got to pull his weight.

I hear the familiar creak-bang, creak-bang from across the street as Mr. Entwistle throws open his window shutters. I know it's nearly time for me to set off because Mr. Entwistle is a man of routine. Same time each day, weekday or weekend—makes no difference to him. Naturally, I have my own routines, and I'm ready to go with the kids' breakfasts boxed up.

After living here for nigh on three years, I know the routines that punch through this building. On a weekday, I know it's time to haul my ass out of bed when my downstairs neighbour slams her front door. I know it's time for my second cup of tea when I hear the orange seller calling from the street. And I know I'm late taking the kids their breakfast when I hear my neighbour's chatterbox child on the stairwell, leaving for school with his quieter older sibling. I like to follow the young boy's fizzing monologue—picking up the odd word or two—as they leave the building and turn down the side alley.

The noisiest time on our street occurs shortly after nine every week-day—when the rubbish and recycling collectors lurch past with their bicycle trailers and empty the bins at the end of each block.

I don't let the boyfriend stay over on Friday night because of my early start. So Saturday morning is altogether quieter. I don't like it. Me, I need distractions—busy, busy, busy. No point dwelling on things, is there? Like how I miss my old life with Ruben, with our bigger flat, our parties. Like how my kid sister fucked up my chances, getting arrested for petty vandalism a month before I was due for brain chipping. That's all it took for *me* to be judged an unsuitable candidate. Why would they enhance someone with suspect genes? The more I ranted my utter frustration, the more my parents told me I was better off staying as I was, like them, fully organic as nature intended.

Come *on*, Caleb. You'd better be up. Maybe he's creeping around trying not to wake the kids. I wouldn't be surprised. He's a considerate, sensitive boy. He's sunny, too, which is surprising, even impressive. I pride myself that those three weeks he spent in my flat—eating regular meals, playing with the kitten—helped him leave his past behind.

If I were more calculating—which I need to be, according to the family—I'd be more guarded. There's no doubt Caleb is a charmer, which can be a dangerous quality. It's easy for a charmer to morph into something darker, a trickster, a con merchant. But the family can't understand; for me, the boy is simply nice to have around. He knows how to get on the right side of me. Acts more like an ally than . . . Well, he knows he's onto a good thing here.

He'll be up and ready, walking around barefoot, waiting for me.

I'll pay Skylark a bonus if Caleb comes good today. A completion bonus. She deserves one not just for finding him but for taking her time to persuade him. It's better that way. They settle in quicker when they feel they've made their own decision. I hope Caleb follows Skylark's example, becomes someone I can trust, someone who's content to work his way up.

When Skylark delivered him, she gave me the backstory without overloading me with detail. She knows I can't get involved with every kid. It's too draining. Even so, poor kid, he lost one parent and then the other. Skylark's best guess was that the mother suffered a breakdown, wandered off—died of exposure—or she was picked up, trafficked.

I haven't pried any further. He's the survivor type, and that's all that matters.

For once, I'll put my foot down with the family, tell them *I'll* make best use of Caleb. He'd be wasted in any other part of the business. And I won't delay. I'll see Jaspar at the family premises later today, and I'll bring up the subject. He makes all the big family decisions these days, so if I persuade *him*, no one else will argue. The last thing I need is Jaspar nicking Caleb off me for heavier work. Caleb has more valuable skills. A case in point—that fur-collared shirt. Nice piece of work. But where did the idea come from?

I pick up the breakfast box for Zach and Mikey and head up the stairs. I unlock and push open the steel door. Soft morning light surges through the stairwell. It's quiet on the roof, and the door to Caleb's hut is closed. Don't say he's still asleep. When I reach the work shed, I find him sat at the table, stitching. He looks up, flashes his smile, and I melt. I leave the kids' breakfast on the shaded side of the work shed.

"Look, Ma Lexie." He whispers, for the kids are still asleep. "I'm covering these buttons with scraps of velvet."

"Leave that. Let's go. We'll get our breakfast in the market." He leaps to his feet. We each take two containers of pressed garments down to the street. I send Caleb back upstairs to fetch coat hangers and finally the tall hand trolley. He runs up, two steps at a time, which warms me. Without being instructed, he stacks the containers on the trolley and grabs the handles. "What's the plan, Ma Lexie?"

"Follow me." I set out towards the market square.

The shutters are pushed back on my sister-in-law's ground-floor flat and I holler, as I always do, through the open window, "Amber!" After a few moments, she appears in the alley.

"Can't stop, Amber, I need extra time for setting up today." I point behind me with my thumb. "Meet my new overseer."

"Got a name?" asks Amber.

"Caleb, madam."

"So, Caleb, you work hard for Ma Lexie today, and I'll invite you for tea and cake on your way home."

He looks at me and back at Amber. "I work hard all the time."

"It's true," I say. "And Caleb's pretty nifty with a needle and thread."

Amber frowns at me, and I know that look. She steps forward to hug me and murmurs, "Come on, Lexie. Let's avoid a rerun, shall we?" She pulls back and adds, "Come out tonight. Listen to the buskers, join the street dancing, hey?"

"No way. Not on a Saturday. I'll be wiped out." She doesn't press me. "Maybe tomorrow," I say. "I won't be so tired after the Sunday market."

We press on, and Caleb calls from behind. "Is she serious, Ma Lexie? About tea?"

"*She* is Miss Amber to you. Show some respect to my late-husband's sister."

"Husband? Late husband?"

I don't answer. For now, I must maintain the distance. As the family keeps harking on: business is business.

Drives me crazy how they watch me. Amber, no doubt, keeps them all informed, though she's kind enough. She knows the sacrifices I made when I married Ruben, that is, when I married *the family*. Even when my Ruben passed away, I didn't contact my parents. Why humiliate myself? They thought I'd married down, seriously down.

Since I was widowed, I admit that Ruben's family has been good to me—setting me up with the flat, the janitor's job and the remake business. It's small-fry to them. I'm definitely grateful; it's not as if Ruben and I had any children. But the way they check on me . . . It's annoying, belittling. And I've no delusions. If I ever remarried, they'd take a different attitude. Kick me out of the flat most likely. So it's best to toe the line. And fair's fair—they don't mind the occasional boyfriend passing through.

"Ma Lexie? Who builds our stall? Did Mr. Ben set things up for you? Do I need to do that now? Is there a clothes—?"

"Too many questions."

The end of our street opens out into the market square with its food stalls, regimented into rows but precariously constructed—old doors and warped planks balanced on crates and blocks. The stall owners are piling up their produce, stringing up multicoloured tarps to offer shade. I wave to the woman who sells fennel—another family widow. I love this time when the market belongs to the stallholders. No shoppers as yet, just the scrawny hangers-on who descend on the food stalls— youngsters mainly, trying to make themselves useful by tautening the canopies, hauling boxes of fruit and vegetables. All unpaid, working for tips. Entrepreneurs in the making, I reckon.

Today, though, I'm on edge. I'm going to put temptation in Caleb's path. Because I need to test his loyalty before I pull him closer. I need to know if he's playing me, if he's all empty charm. I walk faster, stretching the distance between me and the boy; he'll see that I trust him, and he'll taste a bit of freedom. I skirt around the food market and stop by the snack stall at the corner of Clothing Street. It's pushed tight against the end wall of a housing block. I daren't look around in case Caleb isn't there.

He appears beside me. Was he even tempted? Maybe it didn't occur to him. Gingerly, he tilts the trolley upright, with one arm stretched across the top container, stopping it from tipping forward. He looks up to me, expectant.

"Egg wrap?" I ask.

He nods as he studies the handwritten prices. "With sauce," he says. "Please."

"Make that two egg wraps with the extras, and one with sauce," I say to the girl. She splashes oil in the wok, adds onions and herbs from two piles on the counter, cracks two eggs into the mix, whisks, adds spice. "And chilli," I tell her. She takes two thin pittas, spreads one with sauce and splits the egg filling between them.

We stand together eating our breakfast. My shoulders relax. As I look across the market square, I imagine a more traditional scene, with the addition of a church at the far end, and a fountain, and a statue of . . . anyone, for heaven's sake. Anything to relieve the back-to-basics look of the enclave. I know it's a cheap way to live, but does it have to look so bland? The enclave has its graffiti artists who've sprayed the end walls of the housing blocks, but it's all too loud for me. A single tall spire would make all the difference.

In Manchester, if I stayed after work for an hour or two, I'd say to a friend, *Meet you by the Pankhurst statue.* I haven't visited the city since I married my Ruben. I gave up the job, and my free travel pass was revoked automatically. I've never missed the commute, the crammed carriages. And I haven't missed the job. Just another invisible organic working for the bright sparks, the clever bastards. Mind you, having worked with them, seen them up close, I don't envy them, not really. For all their brains—it's not even their *own* brains, it's brain chips making them supercharged—they're no better than skivvies themselves. Talk about a day-in, day-out treadmill, working long hours, hardly seeing home during the week. They don't get it though, do they? All said and done, I wouldn't mind one of their fancy houses in the suburbs—

"Ma Lexie, do I still get pocket money? Or do I get a proper wage now?" He wipes his mouth with the back of his wrist, having finished his wrap already. I've no appetite; I hand him mine, half-finished. He takes it and starts chomping.

I laugh at him. "A wage? What are you worth, Caleb? More than Mr. Ben? Anyway, what do you need money for? I'm feeding you, aren't I? You've got a place to live."

"I think an overseer should get a wage. Not pocket money for sweets."

I laugh again. The cheek of him. Is he judging how far he can push? "You've a short memory. Hmm? Remember when you arrived here? Caked in dirt. Thin as a pin."

"That was then, Ma Lexie. I want to work hard for you, like your sis—like Miss Amber said. And I've plenty more ideas for the workshop, for new remakes."

"There's more to being an overseer than you realise. Mr. Ben made an early start on market days. He collected the boards and trestles from the family premises and set up the stall. I've had to pay one of the family's freelancers to do the job today. That's profit down the drain. You see? So don't talk to me about wages. You haven't proved yourself beyond a bit of handiwork. Be thankful for your breakfast treat."

———

The first of the shoppers are trickling in from the surrounding enclave when Skylark arrives at our pitch. I've finished setting out the garments on the tabletop, and Caleb, with his back to the street, is hanging the most expensive items on the clothes rail.

"What the hell is *that*?" asks Skylark, pointing at the fur-collared shirt.

Caleb spins around. "Skylark!"

"Come here, kid. I've missed your ugly mug."

They're in a bear hug as she says, "What are you doing out here? Got yourself promoted?"

He pulls away. "I'm Ma Lexie's right-hand man."

She grabs him for another hug. "No, you idiot," she says. "I'm the right-hand man. Hey, let's look at you." She steps back, looks him up and down. "Not as skinny." She leans in and inhales. "Smell a bit sweeter too." She puts her arm around him, and it cheers me no end to see Caleb beaming that big smile of his.

Skylark twists around and says, "Ma Lexie, I went to the premises yesterday. Your Mr. Ben's working on the separation line already." She snort-laughs. "He didn't look happy. Not one bit. I couldn't resist— wandered over, all casual, asked him to pick out a fetching frock for me, for a big night out. Told me to fuck off. Still has a way with words."

I turn to Caleb. "Don't just stand around. Tidy up the rails and fasten up all the shirts. They'll blow off the hangers if there's a gust of wind." Taking Skylark by the elbow, I guide her out of the stall, out of earshot. "How was the trip? Anything for me?"

"Sorry, nothing. Pretty tight family groups. A handful of singletons but they were all sick. Anyway, I thought you had enough with three boys."

"We'll see. I might need another, none younger than Caleb though. The young ones need too much organising. Listen, are you busy for the next hour?" Skylark shakes her head. "Take Caleb. Show him around— I'm cutting him some slack—and buy him a toy or a game. I don't know what kids want, and I can't leave the stall."

She gives me that *look*, the same as Amber's. She says, "There's no point spoiling him, getting too close. If Jaspar takes him off your hands like last time, you'll be crying in your soup."

I call Caleb over. Tell him to take a walk with Skylark. He hesitates, looks back and forth between me and Skylark, as if he's suspicious. I explain that I need the stall to myself for half an hour, that a business associate is calling by. I give him a handful of small notes, way more than the usual pocket money, and I watch him swagger away by Skylark's side. I wonder if Skylark has guessed I'm testing the boy. I want to know what he'll do—money in his pocket, out in the market for the first time, his first real chance to make a run for it. After seeing him with Skylark, so relaxed, I reckon there's nothing further from his mind.

———

I hate it when people maul the goods. I can tell they won't buy anything. Take this young woman. Neat as neat can be, shy looking, but a pretty face in a plain way. Somehow she manages to look down her nose at everything on display. And the lad who's with her, he's trying to inject a little enthusiasm. Some folk are born miserable. She holds the cuff of the fur-collared shirt—hanging in pride of place—and she actually cringes. Her shoulders twitch.

God help us. No imagination. No sense of derring-do. What's the matter with people these days? It's all these damned inoculations—no one has any addictions, but these kids growing up now, they're all so damned . . . boring. With our remakes, I can read the confusion in people's faces. They don't know what they want until someone *like me* puts it under their goddamn nose.

The lad is still encouraging her to try something on. She picks up a cap made of army camouflage material with a fluorescent lemon peak—multicoloured metallic beads sewn to the underside. Another of Caleb's ideas. He delegated the beading work to the kids.

She stares at the cap. The lad takes it from her hand and puts it on her head. And she stands in front of my mirror, looking at herself, blank faced. The cap suits her. The lad steps between her and the mirror, bends his knees. He pushes her hair behind her ears and pulls the peak down a tad and pushes it slightly sideways, as though the cap's accidentally off-centre rather than deliberately, cheekily cockeyed. He lifts her chin. It suits her. I'll offer a decent discount for the first sale of the day. Always brings me good luck. But as I step closer, the girl casts the cap aside and they move on. Casts it aside! That's bespoke, lady. It's not jumble.

Speaking of which, I cast a glance farther along Clothing Street. On the opposite side, the second-hand clothes stall is as busy as ever. The clothes are thrown in heaps. But their profits per sale will be tiny compared to mine. I'm not interested in volume trade. If I told Ruben *once*, I told him *twenty* times: the family should develop more spin-offs from the recycling business. What's it called . . . ? An add-on . . . No, *added value*. But Ruben didn't listen. Not the listening type, was he? A real hard worker but, it has to be said, he liked a straightforward job.

God, I miss him though. If he could see me now with my own stall and all these remake fashions, he'd be proud. Ruben's mind fixated on one thing: the weight of recyclables—textiles, metals, glass, plastics, compost. I don't know why he worried. He told me himself that the weigh station staff were paid off. Bumped our weights by twenty per cent.

My Ruben saw himself as the family strongman—keeping rival clans off our street. He patrolled after dark, checking every recycling bin from one end of our street, right across the market square, to the far end of the enclave. He said he needed eyes in the back of his head to stop other street clans from pinching our stuff. He knew every bin on our patch, had them all marked, and checked they were all positioned where they should be. I've pictured him so many times, totally pumped up when he caught them red-handed. I see him, ploughing into them with his baseball bat.

Knifed through the heart for half a bin of metals. My Ruben, bless him, took the small stuff too seriously.

———

Three sales so far. I can't see far along the street; it's thronging. Where the hell are Skylark and Caleb? It must be an hour since they left. I'm aware I'm nibbling at my lower lip.

Why do I do this—set people up to fail? People I actually care about. Jesus, like that time as a teenager. I didn't remind anyone my birthday was coming up. My sixteenth. *Of course*, no one remembered. They were busy, working all hours. My parents felt terrible when they eventually noticed the date. Whereas, for me, I don't know what felt shittiest—everyone forgetting my birthday or seeing everyone's squirming guilt.

I like Caleb. That should be enough. He's well-adjusted and smart, strikes a positive attitude. There's no need to test him like this.

I'll tell the family through Jaspar, in case anyone's in any doubt, that I don't want to remarry. They'll appreciate that, a sign of respect for Ruben's memory. But I want a child—someone I can look after for a few years, who'll look after me in my old age. Frankly, I could simply *do it*: move Caleb into my flat. I could build a platform above the living space for a mattress. I can't have him sleeping in the kitchen. The family will see how happy I am, and Jaspar might be prompted to give me a bigger flat. Or he could encourage the tenant next door to move on and then knock through. That would be grand. Jaspar could make that happen.

Anyway, the family will grasp soon enough that something's going on. Mr. Ben being demoted, Caleb coming to the market. Amber's bound to mention Caleb at the Sunday gathering. Yes, I'll tell Jaspar today that I want to keep Caleb. I'll *tell* him. I won't ask.

I catch sight of Skylark edging, shoulder first, through the crowd. I take payment from a young man for a pair of shorts with bespoke trim on the side seams and pocket edges—a quick job, five minutes with the machine. I fold the shorts, tie them with a thin strip of cloth to make a handle. He doesn't seem too impressed, but it's all part of the service. As he leaves, Skylark darts between the stalls. She's on her own.

"I lost him. At the toy stall in the next street."

"How could you lose—?"

"He ducked down to look in a box of oddments. I don't know, maybe he crawled under the stall and ran from the back end. Couldn't see him. Chased up and down, but—?"

"He ran away?"

"He might be lost, or . . . How much money did you give him?" she asks.

"It's only enclave credits; he won't get far with that."

Skylark lays her hand flat on top of her head. "But he seemed happy. Why run away?"

"Because no one knows who he is yet. It's his first day off the roof. In a month's time everyone will know he's with me."

"Let's not panic," says Skylark. "If he's lost, he'll find his way back to the food market and—"

"Yes, he'll find his way from there."

"I'll keep searching, Ma Lexie. I'll go to the market square, and if he isn't there I'll check if he went home."

As Skylark turns, Caleb crashes into her. "Sorry, Ma Lexie. Sorry. I looked up and I panicked. I couldn't see Skylark." He looks up at her. "Where did you go?"

I lean over and pull him by his top around the table.

"Sorry, Ma Lexie," he whines.

I slap his face.

———

My mother slapped me often enough. It's not the end of the world. But Caleb's been sulking for the past half hour and won't look at me. I sent Skylark to fetch him some toffees, but he hasn't touched them. Pushed them in his pocket. I'm festering with the worst doubts. Did he try to run away but chickened out? I don't know what to think. Did he take his chance and then realise he didn't have a plan? Will he spend the next months working out how to get away? I don't want to be suspicious; I want to believe he lost sight of Skylark and panicked.

We go on like this until late morning: there's me, acting as though nothing has happened, chatting with the customers, pretending Caleb isn't even there; and there's Caleb, standing at the back pretending he's invisible. One of my regulars turns up and we have a laugh. I want Caleb to see that people like me.

A guy I haven't seen before strides up to the stall, points and asks about the shirt. "What kind of fur is it?" I tell him it's mock. And he asks, "Mock what?" I make it up—"Mock arctic fox," I tell him. He says he's doing a music gig, and he'll take it; it's different. I tell Caleb to wrap it nicely. He's watched me wrapping other items, and I reckon he'll enjoy his first sale, if he can get over himself, stop his sulking. He hands over the wrapped shirt and smiles, just about. As the guy heads off, Caleb takes out his toffees and starts to suck on one.

By two o'clock the market is thinning, and I tell Caleb to start packing away. I tell him we've had a good day, thanks to his creative flair. He takes the compliment, and once again tries to smile. It's more like a twitch. I wonder if his face is stinging.

I take a deep breath. "Caleb. Listen to me. I won't hit you again. I was worried and . . . you know, I don't want you to disappear like that. Gave me a fright." I add, "You're important to the business. So, from now on, you'll have a wage instead of pocket money."

He nods his head.

I think we're over the worst.

I say, "We'll go home via the family premises. But first, go back to the fruit market and fetch three pomegranates—a treat for you boys. Go to the woman with the rose tattoo on her throat. Tell her Ma Lexie sent you. And while you're doing that, I'll finish the packing."

I watch him flip-flop down the street. I must be mad, testing him again. But I want him to make good his wrong.

———

We walk back along Clothing Street with the trolley. Instead of turning left towards our housing block, I turn right towards the family premises. At the far end of the street, the housing blocks give way to a shamble of workshops, with perimeter walls, and storage lock-ups, mostly built from recycled plastic building blocks, with battered wooden or steel gates. No signage. Around here, enclave entrepreneurs like to keep a low profile. But the recycling business is different—public contracts and all that—and as we approach the compound walls, I point Caleb to the sign:

MATERIALS RECYCLING FACILITY
ENCLAVE W3
NO DUMPING

"You'll get to know this place, Caleb. It's the family HQ. We keep our bicycle trailers here for the bin collections along our street. And it's the sorting facility for recyclables from the entire enclave—we won the contract a few years back. The family's doing well." I place my hand on his shoulder. "Stick with me and you'll never be short of work."

I look up at the camera, and the gates' unlocking mechanism clunks.

"What happens to the stuff you can't recycle?" Caleb asks. He's perking up.

"We don't bring it here. It's biked out to the incinerators on the eastern edge of the enclave, generates electricity."

The yard is deserted at first sight. The bicycles and trailers are parked up against the perimeter wall. But then I notice there's a mechanic tinkering with one of the bicycles. I avoid coming here during the week when it's chaotic. Frankly, I don't like seeing the boy who once worked for me—the one Jaspar purloined. Haven't seen him in a while. Makes me feel bad he's doing such dirty work. Within months he was unrecognisable, changed shape with all the cycling and heavy lifting. At least if he's still on the collection side, he's not sorting in the warehouse—too hot in the summer, too cold in the winter—and it's pure bedlam in there with the conveyors, rolling drums, air blowers, sorting screens. First time I went in, I threw up.

"Caleb, I need to talk business with my brother-in-law. You run over to the warehouse, have a rummage in the textile bay." I point to the near end of the warehouse. "There's a security guard. Say you're here with Lexie."

He stares at me, quizzical. "Have a rummage?"

"It's part of your new job. Bag up the best and we'll take it home. Don't see why I should do it any longer. I couldn't ask Mr. Ben to do it; he had no idea. Now, off you go."

"But how much—?"

"Whatever you can balance on the trolley."

I head off towards the office—a windowless steel shipping container. We keep a strongbox welded to the floor, and it's the safest place to leave my takings. I don't want cash lying around at home. I've gleaned that my latest Romeo has a limited understanding of *what's mine isn't yours*. He's had the nerve to drop hints about moving in with me. The next thing you know, he'll be saying, *Let's share and share alike.* I don't care that he's lazy, as long as it doesn't affect me. I'm nobody's meal ticket. My Ruben would climb out of the grave.

Jaspar steps out of the office, looks across at the warehouse as Caleb parks his trolley and disappears inside. "The kid. I could do with an extra pair of hands on the sorting line. Can you spare him?"

"He's too smart for this work, Jaspar. He's better staying with me. He's doing nice work, proper designer in the making."

"Fancy that," he says, all sarcastic. He smirks. "*This*"—he waves towards the warehouse—"*this* is where the family makes its money.

Where there's muck etcetera. Your *operation*, if I may raise it to that lofty status—"

"Don't patronise me, Jaspar. If you need more hands, tell Skylark and pay her a bonus if she delivers."

"Just saying. Keep your hair on."

"Well, I'm telling you, the boy's staying with me. I'm paying him a wage from today, so don't fucking mess with my plans."

He rolls his eyes. "Calm it, yeah? And this is strictly business, is it? Tell me, if I took him, would we have them tears again?"

"That was two years ago. I was still in a bad way after Ruben. So, hands up, I overreacted." I pass the takings to him. He retreats into the office, and I call after him. "I admit, I like this boy, but it makes real business sense to keep him."

"I've told you: don't mix business and personal shit."

"It's all right for you, Jasp. Married with four lovely kids. My marrying days are over. Ruben was the only one for me." I hate to use Ruben like this. It's still difficult for his family, especially for Jaspar, losing his kid brother.

After Ruben's murder, the enclave police weren't too bothered about following up—regarded it as clan business—so we did our own investigating. Asked every resident what they'd thrown in the stolen metals' bin, and we made an inventory of everything the residents could remember. Jaspar's unloading team at the yard inspected every delivery of metals for weeks and weeks against that inventory. Four months on, we spotted a small wire sculpture of a dog that some old fella had made and discarded to the stolen bin. Jaspar went to see him with what we'd found, and he confirmed it was the one he'd chucked away. According to the delivery records, the wire dog arrived at the recycling yard from the far side of the enclave, from a collection gang that had *previous form* for pilfering, according to Jaspar. By then, the police had long forgotten about my Ruben. They didn't make the connection when the retributions started. More than one tit for one tat. But that's how it goes.

Jaspar locks the strongbox and continues his needling. "We don't want no embarrassment for the family. The kid's a migrant, could be anyone. We've no idea what he's gone through, what he might do. Might be a ticking time bomb for all we know. And I'll tell you another thing for free." He steps towards me and grabs my arm tight, doesn't let go. "I don't like that fucken loser you're seeing. Don't look good." He juts out his chin, spoiling for a punch. I come dangerously close to laughing at the jerk, even though he's hurting me. He lets go of my arm. God, it stings.

"I'm finishing with him, Jasp. I got lonely, that's all."

"Don't *you* finish with the loser. *I'll* put him straight. We don't want no shouting match for the neighbours to blab about. Do we?"

"And I can keep the boy?"

"Yeah. Keep the little bastard, if he's that special."

———

Caleb returns from the warehouse with two large bundles of clothing—one gathered up in a blanket, the other in a torn sheet. He balances them on the trolley as best he can, but it's obvious I'll have to carry one of them. I'm wondering if his face will be bruised by morning.

"Why so much, Caleb? That's easily twice as much as we need for one week."

The bundles slip off.

"It's a new idea, Ma Lexie." He still sounds a bit downbeat, but at least he's talking.

"Please do share," and I'm surprised at the sarcasm in my voice. Jaspar brings out the worst in me. I add, trying to sound calm, "I'd like to know."

"I'm going to cut up eight or nine pairs of trousers to make one or two pairs of remake trousers."

"What?"

"They're worthless right now."

"Why nine pairs—surely two or three—swap the pockets, that sort of thing?"

"This is different. I'll cut them in curves and piece them together like a curvy-edged jigsaw."

"Too much stitching."

"It's all machine work. No hand stitching."

"Make the fur-collared shirts first. After that, I'll give you one day to make a sample for me. *One day*, are you listening? Then I'll decide if we'll begin a new line." As an afterthought, for I can see his face is indeed still red from the slap, and his forehead is creased as if he has a headache, I say, "I'd like to start a new line of specials. I'll give you one day every week for developing new ideas. Agreed?" He nods and, at last, a smile, though it's strained and fleeting. "We'll get the kids to make labels and stitch them on the outside of the clothes." I turn towards the metal entrance gates, and so I don't see his reaction when I say, "We'll call it the Caleb fashion line."

He doesn't reply.

There's a ruckus outside—kids screaming, playing some stupid chasing game. I walk on ahead, back towards the centre of the enclave, but I twist around because I can't hear the trolley squeaking. He's standing stock-still, staring at the kids. They're chasing one another with sticks, there's a ball in there somewhere, and they're kicking up clouds of dust.

I call to him. "Come on. Remember? Cake?"

———

I'm too tired to walk to the shower block down our street. I close the kitchen shutters, strip off and fill the sink with warm water. Caleb's gone back to the roof with the food we picked up on the way home, taken the pomegranates too. Should I have taken the keys away from him? I'm pretty sure I can trust him. He's keen to sew the remake trousers. And I don't want him to feel demoralised, which he would be if I took the keys. I have to assume, for the time being, that he told the truth about losing sight of Skylark. He panicked, that's all.

I'm free for the rest of the evening. I should be happy with the day—trade was brisk, and Jaspar agreed to let me hold on to Caleb. What's more, I have the beginnings of a real plan—a new line in remakes. I'll sketch some ideas for the label's design. Could be the start of a bigger business, because I see no reason why I shouldn't expand, supply other enclaves. If the business does take off big-time, I'll give up the janitor's job. It makes far more sense to rent a workshop near the family premises.

I take my washing cloth, an old, thin hand towel, and soak it in the warm, soapy water. I wring it, but not too tight, shake it out and throw it across my back. A satisfying slapping sound bounces off the kitchen walls. Pulling the cloth back and forth, I start to feel cooler. Slowly, I wipe myself down. I stand still enjoying the goose bumps. Leaning over the sink, I rinse my face with fresh water from the tap, pull a strand of hair across my face and inhale. The cloying smell of the recycling yard lingers. I put my head under the running tap.

————

I sit cross-legged on my bed. The bedsheet is scattered with dashed-off sketches for a "Caleb" logo. He'd like this one. I pick up the outline of a leaping cat.

At Amber's place this afternoon, he instantly recognised her marmalade cat when it jumped in through the window from the street. There's no mistaking its markings—a white front leg and white chest. Caleb pointed, dumb, his mouth full of cake. I explained, "Yes, I borrowed the cat while you settled in. But she lives here."

I couldn't believe it. His eyes filled with tears. Acted like a baby. He slid down on to the floor and played with the cat for the rest of our stay. I felt embarrassed by him, so I deflected Amber before she passed comment. I could see the start of a sneer. I leaned towards her, told her my boyfriend was getting his marching orders, that Jaspar insisted on "handling the situation."

She said, "That's probably wise."

Caleb paid no attention to us. Amber shifted closer and told me she'd never liked the boyfriend, thought he was annoyingly flippant, as though he didn't need to earn a living like everyone else. Got up her nose, she said, the way he took advantage of my good nature. "You've got to stop this—forever seeing the best in people."

I said, "Well, I didn't make a mistake with your brother Ruben, did I?" Which she could have taken as a compliment if she cared to. Past caring. All said and done, she'd never piped up about lover boy before now.

No point getting het up. I know I've had my best years.

I never felt too tired to go out dancing with Ruben. I feel his hand on my waist and glimpse the roll of his hips. He was some dancer.

In reality, I had no great qualms walking away from my own family, but I never thought I'd end up here. Like this. If we'd had children, I might have patched things up with my own parents. I suppose it's possible they're looking, even now, to end the rift. People can't stay angry forever.

Unless they don't even think of me. I draw an outline of a cat with a bird in its mouth. I might be dead to them already.

CHAPTER 3

CALEB

As Zach spreads out the raffia mat, Mikey shoots questions at me about my first day off the roof. He wants to know how far it is to the market, if Ma Lexie let me serve on the stall. And he pesters me to ask Ma Lexie if he and Zach can go next time. As I answer one question, he's interrupting with the next. I hold my hands up to say: *Enough.*

Zach, quiet so far, chips in with one question: "Did you see any stalls selling figs?" I'm not surprised he asks me this. He told me one time that his family had fig trees, but when I asked how many, he didn't know. It's possible his family owned a whole fig farm. *Or,* just as likely, Mikey remembered a small garden at his family home—two or three fig trees planted for shade as well as fruit. I felt sad that he remembered so little. I explain to Zach that I didn't have time to look around the fruit stalls, but there must be figs somewhere, and I'll try to buy some at tomorrow's market if Ma Lexie lets me.

He says, "I like figs more than sweets."

We sit ourselves down, picnic-style again, and I hand out the spicy egg wraps. It was my idea to buy the street food on our way home. I told Ma Lexie, "You must be too tired to cook. You've had a busy day."

Honest, I couldn't care less about Ma Lexie being tired. I was worried about Zach and Mikey, who would be starving hungry. During the weekend markets, they go without food at midday—there's no one around to feed them. Buying street food was the quick way to get the kids fed.

I put on a brave face—same as I did at Jaspar's recycling yard—because I can't admit to the kids that I've been in trouble with Ma Lexie. I pretend everything's okay by telling them about the amazing sight at the far end of Clothing Street. I saw it when I walked through the market with Skylark: a massive pink sheet was strung up between two buildings on opposite sides of the street. It blew around in the breeze high above the stalls, like a giant advertisement saying *Welcome to Clothing Street*. I explain to Zach and Mikey that most of the stalls sold second-hand clothes, piled high, but Ma Lexie's stall looked special. "We should feel proud of that," I say, making a real effort to sound happy. My fur-collared shirt, I tell them, sold to a musician for a sky-high price, and he didn't even barter.

And I give them the gossip, that Ma Lexie was married one time, that she's widowed now.

I describe Miss Amber's flat and the cat with the incredible coat of fur—orange with one patch of white on its front leg. I told them I'd seen the cat before, when it was smaller, when I first arrived at Ma Lexie's flat. I tell them that I'm sure the cat remembered me because she curled up in my lap like we were old friends. But I don't tell Zach and Mikey about Miss Amber's cake because I don't want them to feel jealous.

And I don't tell them that Ma Lexie hit me.

I've never been hit across the face before. My parents never ever smacked me. The inside of my mouth still stings, but at least I can't taste blood any longer. After the slap, Ma Lexie joked around with her customers like nothing had happened, and Skylark gave me toffees, as if toffees would make everything all right. I thought I'd be sick if I tasted anything sweet, but in the end my mouth was hurting so much I tried one, and it did ease the pain a little. Then, out of nowhere, Ma Lexie said she wouldn't hit me again. I wanted to tell her that no one in my family ever hit another person, that she was bad. Instead, I clamped my mouth shut and imagined a blade in my hand. I saw myself lunging at her.

And I know I'll be ready, if only with my fist, if she ever does that again in front of people, in front of Skylark.

I expected a telling-off after I gave Skylark the slip, but Ma Lexie should have believed my story. So, I learned an important lesson today. It took me a while to work it out. My head was ringing. While I stood at the back of the stall, I decided Ma Lexie didn't trust me—even though I'd worked hard and tried to be cheerful all the time. I never once blamed her for any of my problems. I decided, standing there listening to her laughing and joking with her scummy customers, that Ma Lexie is just another chapter in my story of hard luck.

When I saw the cat at Miss Amber's, I lost it. I couldn't hold back all the sadness. I had to dive off my chair to hide my tears. What with Ma Lexie hitting me, and with the warning from the guard at Jaspar's warehouse. The guard said, "Don't get too cosy with that boss of yours. The last one she took a shine to was *confiscated* by Jaspar. Started on collections. Ended up here on the sorting lines. But the kid got on Jaspar's wick. Shipped him out."

I don't know why, but I said to the security guard, "Thanks for telling me." And he replied, "No skin off my nose."

As usual when we sit on our mat, I make sure I'm facing Odette's roof. I like to watch her move in and out of the garden as she takes drinks to the visitors. When she isn't busy, she stands quietly, all watchful. I'm sure she chooses a place to stand where she can look across to my roof. One of the things I like about her, at least from a distance, is that she always looks so clean. Her dark hair is neat, scraped back in a ponytail.

I stand up. "Save the pomegranates for later, boys, or you'll be hungry again before bedtime."

Mikey clears away the food wrappers, and Zach rolls up the mat while I walk across to the edge of the roof and wave to Odette. She doesn't move. I guess she's being careful, in case her boss or the visitors are watching her. I head off to the work shed to sort through the recycled clothing I brought home from the warehouse. While I'd rummaged in the textile bay, I picked out two warm tops for myself and buried them deep in the bundles. I've learned to plan ahead like this. The days will be getting shorter soon, and with these warm clothes I won't wake up in the night, freezing cold.

I carry the tops back to my hut and hang them from the hooks under the shelf. I like the look of them. It's good to have something new.

———

I take off my T-shirt and wash at the sink. It's odd; it's a relief to be back on the roof where I can reach up and almost touch the big blue sky. Down on the street—this came as a surprise—I felt the buildings were leaning in, that they could easily topple over and bury me.

As I turn away from the sink, I see Odette, waving—not in a *nice to see you* way, but in a way that says *hurry up, I need you*. I cock my head. What's the big panic? She pretends she's throwing a bottle and waves towards herself.

She wants the torch, but why the drama? I should tell her about the trouble her stupid errand dropped me in.

Skylark took me to the toy stall, and on the way I saw a pile of gadgets, mostly junk, and I spotted a solar torch. I should have told Skylark I wanted to buy it, but something told me to keep quiet. If she'd asked me why I wanted one, I didn't have an answer. Because, here on the roof, there's light from the streetlamps. And I couldn't say I wanted the torch for Odette. Skylark would have too many questions about that.

When we reached the toy stall, I waited until Skylark looked away, and I ducked down, retraced our route, bought the torch and ran back. I'd been gone for a couple of minutes, that's all, but Skylark had disappeared. I raced around the stall, looked down an alley that led away from the market, hoping to spot her. The alley stretched away into the distance. I don't know why I did it, but I took a few steps, and then I ran as if the alley sucked me along. I wanted to run, to find the end—where the enclave meets the countryside. It felt good—to be on my own and running. I'd run half the length of the alley when I came to my senses and ran all the way back, straight to Ma Lexie's stall.

I wrap the torch in a cloth, push it into a wide-necked container and add more padding for a snug fit. On a scrap of paper, I write, *What's the panic?* The container is heavier than the usual bottle. Odette's waving, encouraging me to throw. I hold it up and gesture that it's heavy. She puts her hand to her forehead; she thinks I'll fail. I practise a longer run-up, and feeling confident, I run—counting the steps—and launch the container, higher than usual.

She reaches, and with her fingertips she manages to break the container's fall. She rushes off, out of sight, and I'm left wondering what she's up to. I sit and watch.

———

The sun is low, and I'm ready to flop out. I can hear Zach and Mikey playing at the far end of the roof. I'm relieved they haven't pestered me to join in. I'm suddenly reminded of the older boys and girls playing outside the family premises this afternoon. As soon as I heard them screaming for the ball, memories washed over me. For a couple

of seconds, I was standing in my street back home, on the sidelines
watching my friends running around. Seemed such a long time since
I'd seen a sweaty, shoulder-barging, shirt-grabbing ball game of any
kind. But it hit me that this enclave game had a nasty edge to it. Each
kid had a stick like a stripped branch, and it seemed—but it was difficult to believe—that they were using them to hit *one another* rather
than the ball. I'd never seen anything like these sticks—hand-painted
as if in team colours, either pale blue or yellow, with coloured stripes
around the shafts.

———

Still no sign of Odette. I might have missed her; there's only the street-
light now. I thought she'd send me a message, thank me for the torch.
She hasn't even asked how much I paid for it. Unless she thinks I stole
it. I guess she wants a torch for when the days become shorter. Maybe
she wants a better light for reading. Or she's afraid of the dark, and
when autumn comes—when it's too cold to sleep under the stars—she
plans to fall asleep in her hut under torchlight. I can't blame her; since
I crossed the Channel to England, everyone seasick, in total darkness—

The steel door creaks open on her roof, and I see the silhouette of
Odette's boss, a stooped woman who always dresses in black. I think
she's carrying a plate of food. She disappears into the garden. I guess
she'll leave Odette's meal near her hut.

After a couple of minutes, she hasn't reappeared. They must be
chatting. Thinking about it, Odette doesn't say much about her boss
in her messages.

I decide to crash out, accepting that Odette will chat away the entire
evening without messaging me. As I turn away, I catch, in the corner of
my eye, a darting movement on her roof. I look across. She darts again,
stops suddenly and runs in my direction. She throws a bottle and it flies

way over my head, landing on the far side of the roof. Ha, she's overdone that! I chase across and find the bottle perched over the roof drain. I use two hands to lift it, carefully—I don't want to nudge it down the drain. I'm still feeling pleased with myself as I open the bottle and read the message: *I am leeving NOW. Going to the hills. Come with me. Only 1 chance.*

I'm staring, reading and rereading these four strange sentences.

Going to the hills?

I see myself sprinting down the alley this afternoon. It felt good.

Only one chance?

I poke the inside of my cheek with my tongue. It still hurts. Ma Lexie hit me hard. And I know she'll do it again.

All's quiet in the work shed. I glance across. I can't help Zach and Mikey. I just *can't.*

And *if* I'm going to run away, I know what to take.

Odette approaches the rail, and I walk forward so we face one another. She raises her hand and spreads her fingers wide. I think she's *signalling* . . . five minutes.

I return the signal and feel every hair stand on end. I imagine meeting her in the street. I'll see her smile, close-up.

There's a sudden buzzing in my ears and it's deafening. I swallow hard. My legs are heavy, as if my feet are caked in mud. I walk slowly towards my hut even though I haven't made up my mind. I can decide while I'm packing.

It's a lesson I learned on the road. When there's an emergency, the ones who survive best are the ones who think and act immediately, who don't wait to see what other people do. I'm tipping everything out of my backpack as I focus my thoughts on winter weather, cold nights, wet feet. Before I start to repack it, I change my shorts for trousers, flip-flops for socks and shoes. Into the backpack, I place the two warm tops—Odette might need one—Mother's sewing kit, a spare pair of shoes. My documents are still safe inside the backpack's straps.

I step outside, go around the back of the hut and pull out, as quietly as I can, a scuffed green tarp, and I fold it. I place it inside the backpack as an extra waterproof layer—an old habit—to protect my clothes. I add my hat even though it's smelly, all my socks and a couple more T-shirts. Almost done. I have one thin plastic cape, which I fold and push into a side pocket. I've no food, only a pack of toffees. But I have money in the straps of my pack, and I pray that Odette is better prepared.

I sit and hug my pack. My eyes are closed.

I find myself on my feet, my pack over my shoulder, and I'm stepping out of the hut. I close the hut door so it doesn't creak or bang shut during the night. There's an empty bottle by the parapet wall. I take it over to the sink and fill it with water, push it in a side pocket.

My ears are still ringing. Five minutes must be up by now, but I can't see Odette. I haven't heard her opening the steel door. Maybe she can see me—our roof is more open than theirs. I remove my shoes and tiptoe across to the work shed. There's no sound coming from the kids, and when I look in, I see their shapes under their blankets.

The question is: Can I unlock the steel door and open it without alerting Ma Lexie? The sound of women laughing and shouting reaches me from somewhere in the neighbourhood. I wait, rest my head against the warm steel. When the women reach our building, still shouting, I turn the key, ease the door open and squeeze through. The women's laughter echoes up the stairwell, which is open at ground level to the street—there's no entrance door on any of the enclave housing blocks. I tell myself there's nothing but fresh air between me and the street.

If Ma Lexie has heard a suspicious noise, she'll be listening carefully. So I don't lock the door behind me. Quickly, gripping my shoes, I pass Ma Lexie's flat. Down, down, and one flight from the entrance, I stop, push my feet back into my shoes and wait.

I could turn around even now.

If Odette isn't waiting for me, I'll go back. The door to the roof is still unlocked. Ma Lexie wouldn't hear anything.

From the street, I hear "Caleb!" I can't see her, but I rush down the final steps. She appears at the entrance, a face of stone, and with a head jerk, tells me to follow. Not as prim-looking close-up. Her ponytail is skew-whiff, and strands of oily hair have come loose.

Four or five paces behind her, I'm panicking—we look all wrong. Me with my backpack, wearing trousers and shoes on a hot night, and Odette with a small but bulging bag with a long strap cutting into her shoulder. She's wearing a dress and flip-flops, not exactly escape gear. I've got a bad feeling.

There's an alley up ahead leading off the street. I rush forward, grab Odette's arm and pull her into the alley, saying, "I'm known down that street—Ma Lexie's sister lives there."

"Okay, okay," she snaps. "But we must go in that direction soon." She looks at me. "You're younger than I thought."

"Where are we going?"

"Head south, find the canal path, head to Wales. You're my half brother—got it?"

I'm massively relieved. She has a plan and a story. "Got any food?"

"Some. Enough."

There's a lump deep in my chest. "Let's run."

"No! Look normal."

"What do we say if—?"

"No one's going to stop us. It's Saturday night. Any police will stay close to the market square," she says.

"How did you get away? I didn't see your boss."

But she ignores me. "Walk slowly—like we're tired, near the end of a long walk." After a few seconds: "Thanks for the torch."

"How far is Wales? Where—?"

"Not sure. We'll walk at night, sleep during the day."

"But what happens in Wales? Is it any better than here?"

She ignores me again. "Let's go another two blocks down the alley, then turn south."

"But, how do you know where the canal is?"

She keeps her head down as she says, "People come to the garden. They chat. One old man worked on the canals, talks about the old days. I know if we walk south we will find a canal."

"We won't miss it?"

"Impossible. There are two canals that meet, and the enclave sits in a V between them. See? It's simple, we keep walking south, across two or three fields."

Two or three fields doesn't sound too bad. And now I click—it's totally sensible to leave in the summer, in dry weather. We've had no rain for over three weeks. It's a clear night, too, so we'll follow the stars like Mother and I did. Odette turns off the alley. The enclave is built on a grid, and this street will take us away from the market square.

———

We've been walking for at least twenty minutes. We've passed a few people, but no one seems to eye us up. I'm beginning to think this is easy when three men exit a building about fifty paces ahead of us, and even at that distance I see their swagger. Odette sees them too. She takes my elbow, pushes me through the entrance to a block of flats and marches me up the first flight of stairs. She whispers, "Wait." She's still gripping my elbow, as if I might run off, but when the men have walked by, she releases me and we set off again.

She stops when we reach the last housing block. Before us lies a mess of workshops and shacks, with no streetlights.

"Watch for dogs," I say. "Pick up a stick if you see one."

Dropping her bag to the ground, she pulls out a dark sweater, full of holes, and pulls it over her head. She pulls on baggy black trousers, swaps her flip-flops for shoes and tucks her dress inside the trousers.

While she's doing this, I'm losing my nerve. I'm confused. Why did she ask me to come with her? Am I being stupid? She's not my friend, not really—not like a friend back home. Also, she's older than I thought. She might be eighteen.

In my mind, I walk our route in reverse through the enclave. There's nothing to stop me from changing my mind. I could walk back, climb the stairs, reach my overseer's hut before Ma Lexie has even gone to bed for the night. She'd have no idea. I could then think more clearly, make a sensible decision about my future. I could even plan another escape, when I'm better prepared. I have the key, after all. I could go anytime. Why go tonight with Odette?

A short heavy man—looks like a weightlifter—walks one slow step after another along the perimeter wall of the nearest workshop. We wait. He passes by and heads into the enclave along the next street. My heart is thumping. Would I feel braver a year from now? Yes, much braver, I'm sure of it, and I could make my escape without any help. But Ma Lexie will surely hit me many times before then. Or she'll take away my key—especially when she hears that Odette has escaped. And what if she has an argument with Jaspar? He'd steal me from Ma Lexie to teach her a lesson.

Odette steps out and heads across the open ground. I hesitate and stare at her back as she heads towards darkness. I step out and follow.

We're jogging, sticking close to the perimeter walls of the workshops. If I felt scared while dodging through the enclave alleys and streets, I feel ten times worse now. Mother and I often walked at night, so I know how dark it can be a few metres from a lit street. We're lucky there's a three-quarter moon tonight.

———

Beyond the rough edge to the enclave, Odette takes the solar torch from her bag. "I already checked it," she says. "It works."

"Don't switch it on. Not this close to the enclave," I tell her.

"I'm not stupid."

My fingertips tingle. She's spitting her words at me because she's worried. It's nerves. I'm sure. But it dawns on me that I made a mistake five months ago when I first saw Odette. It's possible that I've confused Odette with Gina, back home, who also had dark hair pulled back in a ponytail. At a distance they looked similar. I think Gina liked me, even though she was much smarter. And I liked her because she wasn't a show-off. She'd look surprised in class when she gave the right answer. Odette is nothing like Gina.

Leaving the workshops way behind, we cross open ground and reach a deserted road. No headlights in sight. Hardly anyone owns a car in the enclave—not Ma Lexie. I didn't see a car at the family premises. I guess Jaspar doesn't have one either.

It all seems a long time ago—Mother and Father taking me on day trips to the coast. They sold our car to my mother's friend. She came to our flat with the cash, and I went to my bedroom; I couldn't bear to see Mother hand over the keys.

When Father set out on his long journey, Mother insisted he should take most of the cash from selling the car. But by the time Mother made up her mind that *we* should leave—the taps had run dry for two months, and bowser water had become expensive—we found we couldn't sell anything, none of our furniture or electrical stuff, because so many people had already left. I gave all my games to the few friends who were still around.

Mother spent three days making preparations, packing our backpacks, then unpacking and repacking. I remember the moment she locked the door to our flat. She stood there for two whole minutes, her head against the door, before she withdrew the key from the lock. The queues at the bus station went around the ticket hall three times, and the price of the tickets had doubled since Father left. The bus took us close to the border. That's when we started walking. We couldn't take a bus or a train across—we'd be sent back at the first checkpoint.

Men in open trucks were offering lifts, but Mother said, "Don't trust anyone, Caleb. We know where we're headed as long as we stay on our own two feet."

Odette and I stand side by side on the potholed tarmac, facing an overgrown hedge.

She says, "We need to get off the road. There's too much moonlight."

I nod my head. We set off walking along the road. Odette soon picks up the pace. We must have jogged a kilometre when the road veers, and on the bend there's a field gate. We climb onto the middle bar and stare ahead, looking roughly south. I wonder if Odette knows how lucky we are—the field is unploughed. It could be grazing land, but I don't see any cowpats. Without speaking a word, we climb over, and that's when I point out the North Star.

Halfway across the field, I call to her. "Odette? Wait. I want to know something." She doesn't stop or even slow down. I'm four or five paces behind her. "Why did you ask me to run away with you? You could have escaped without me."

She carries on walking but shouts over her shoulder: "It's safer with two. And it's not safe for me, a girl."

"But what can I—?"

She shouts: "It's just not safe!" She suddenly stops and twists around. "I thought you were older . . . *I'll* be looking after *you*. That was *not* the plan."

———

Without the stars, we'd be lost. We'd be wandering around within the V-shaped land between the two canals. The fields are odd shapes. It would be easy to think we were sticking to a southerly direction when, in truth, we were heading off in an arc.

We've crossed five fields. The second and third were wheat fields, so we walked the perimeters where the farmers have left strips of grassland a few metres wide—overgrown but still an easier path than crossing the furrows. We climb a stile and find ourselves in yet another wheat field. Odette turns and looks up, checks the North Star again and says, "I'm tired, Caleb, but we can't stop. We must find the canal tonight."

"Let's hope we don't meet a river. The nearest crossing could be miles away."

Her blank face tells me she doesn't want to hear this.

———

We reach the eighth or ninth field, and the land falls away towards the south into woodland. I have a good feeling. I stride out, take the lead and, all the time, I'm saying to myself that our escape will succeed. It *has* succeeded. Ma Lexie will be fast asleep. She won't ever see me again, because I'm guessing Ma Lexie and the family can't tell the police I've disappeared. I think they'd be in trouble. Will they even bother to look for me?

There's a waist-high, barbed-wire fence running along the woods. We throw our bag and backpack across, and I hold the wire down while Odette stretches over. Her trousers snag but she pulls herself free and clambers over, loses her footing and crashes into the ground. She laughs. I laugh with her. She struggles back to her feet and holds down the wire for me.

We wait, our eyes adjusting to the darkness within the woods. I startle as an owl's hoot cuts through the rustling leaves. A more distant owl hoots in reply. Odette is ready to switch on the torch, but we stand still and listen as the owls hoot to one another across the woodland. I hope Odette is thinking the same as me—that the risks we are taking are worth it, right now, at this very moment. She shines the torch towards the ground, and we step over exposed roots and fallen branches, slowly making our way into the heart of the woods.

I heard a story once, on the road, of a night just like this when five friends walked through a forest looking for a safe route, wanting to avoid the roads as we do tonight. The five friends kept real close, or they thought they kept close, but when they reached the end of the forest only four of them walked out. So I decide to walk one pace behind Odette. Not that I'm panicking. I've walked through woods as dark as this before.

She stops and switches off the torch. I step forward to stand side by side with her. She points over to our left. "We're near the edge," she says. "I'm sure of it." She switches the torch on, and we press ahead. And suddenly we're in semidarkness, the trees thin out, and I catch sight of the moon. As we climb up an embankment, I look up to a star-filled sky. We reach flat ground. In front of us, the still water of a canal.

Which canal, I've no idea. Odette puts her arm around me, squeezes my shoulder. I think she'll be kinder now that she's less worried. "We should rest a while, Caleb, eat a bit of food, then walk along the canal path until first light."

As if we both hold the same fear, that the stars and moon will betray us, we step carefully down the embankment. I sit on my backpack while Odette digs around inside her bag for food. She hands me the torch. "Shine it in here." She pulls out two oranges and a bar of chocolate, and she sits down. I shine the torchlight on her hands as she places the oranges on the ground. She breaks the chocolate bar in half and hands me my share. I see, in bright detail, the thumbnail of her right hand, the half-moon of her nail and the thin lines that run from the half-moon to the thumbnail tip.

I see something else.

I take the chocolate, then track her hand with the torchlight. She passes me an orange. It sits in her palm. And I delay a moment in taking it. I squint, looking hard at her fingernails.

"Switch it off," she says. "We don't need the light."

I've seen enough to kill my appetite. A thin line of blood under each nail. I've seen my own fingernails in that state after I've stitched a bad wound. I flick the torchlight up towards her neck, see a smear of blood under her right ear.

"Switch it off, will you?" She punches my shoulder.

I don't dare to peel the orange. My hands are shaking too much. I place the orange in my trouser pocket, telling Odette I'll eat it during the walk. I eat the chocolate, but I don't taste a thing.

She asks, "What time will your boss know you're gone?"

"Six thirty." On Sundays, I tell her, Ma Lexie gets up early for market, but not as early as she does on Saturday.

Odette says that we must walk at least ten miles before daylight. Tomorrow night we must walk at least twenty. That way, we should reach Wales and the border country in two or three nights. She must be guessing. She admitted earlier she didn't know the distance. But why quiz her? It's pointless. When we get there, she says, there'll be plenty of work on the farms and orchards, picking fruit, picking grapes. "We can enjoy the open air and spend all day chatting with the other pickers. I'm fed up with no one to talk to." She picks up the torch and shines it straight into my face. "Why so quiet, Caleb?" She frowns at me. "You can't go back. You know that, don't you?"

I lift my hand to shield my eyes. I know the truth now. She's not my friend. I don't think she ever was. "I don't want to go back. I want to go to Wales."

———

Now that I'm walking along the canal path about twenty paces behind Odette, I replay everything that happened on her roof this evening. Her boss, the old woman, came to the roof with the plate of food. She disappeared from view, and I didn't see her reappear. Next . . . Odette ran across the roof, and that was when she threw the bottle with the message. Then, Odette came to the edge of her roof and signalled to me: *five minutes.*

I'm in trouble if I stay with Odette. I'm guessing . . . in a few hours, she'll be wanted for murder. And Odette, I suspect, needs me for cover. The police will be looking for a girl on her own. Not a girl and a boy. They won't be looking for a boy at all. Because Ma Lexie will keep her mouth shut about me.

———

The canal surface reminds me of a metal ruler stretching into the distance, silver in the moonlight. I tick off the distance by counting my steps. It distracts me from thinking about how tired I am. The walk is easy, as walks go, but I'm aching because although I'm stronger than I used to be—thanks to the food at Ma Lexie's—I've lost all the stamina I built up while walking with Mother. You get into a rhythm. You let go of time.

I try to imagine myself with my old friends walking through the countryside close to home. Instead of Odette, I see Leo up ahead. We've slipped out of our homes for a midnight adventure, and we'll return safely to our beds. We pretend we're the resistance and special combat troops, working together to blow up bridges. Never in a million years would we pretend we're escaping migrants, with no real plan, no real destination.

In the moonlight, single oak trees stand like sentries positioned across the countryside. In the middle distance, there's a security light by a farm building. The only sounds are our footsteps on the gravel path, the swishing of treetops in the breeze and, once so far, a dog barking in a farmyard.

I try to keep my thoughts in a straight line. Don't ask Odette any questions. There's no point asking her about the smear on her neck or her fingernails. I can't trust anything she says. Maybe she wants me along until we're close to Wales, and then she'll give me the slip. If the police find us together, I'll be in as much trouble as her. But *I've* done nothing wrong.

A long line of narrow boats is moored to the bank up ahead. Odette waits for me to catch up and says, "Walk on the grass edge, slowly. Stay close." We tread past, one deliberate step after another. Pots of geraniums have been placed on the roof of one narrow boat. I'm sure people are living inside. There's an empty bottle of wine in the bow of another. My backpack catches on a long bramble and makes a loud scratching noise as I tug myself free. I stop, look over my shoulder, check I'm clear of the bramble and press on. We stay on the grass until we've left the moorings far behind.

———

The sky starts to get lighter, and the thin mist that hangs over the canal and surrounding fields won't hide us for much longer. I've already heard a tractor. For the past two miles, I've looked for places to hide out. There are gaps in the hedges along the canal path, but they all lead into fields. Even if we tried to sleep in a deep furrow, or under the hedgerow, we could be spotted by farmworkers.

The path takes us under a brick-built bridge, and Odette says we'll bed down as soon as we find cover. I'm beginning to wish we'd stopped an hour ago. We've passed cottages with long gardens reaching down to the canal side. One had a garden shed, close to the canal. I pointed it out to Odette, said we could break into the shed and sleep there. She shook her head. No discussion. I've also seen a clump of trees in the middle of a field, but I think they've grown around a pond.

About fifteen minutes' walk beyond the road bridge, we come to a good spot where a patch of woodland reaches the path—like the woodland at the start of our canal walk.

"Here," she says. We walk thirty or forty paces off the path until we come across a small dip. She says, "I need a pee. Turn around."

The ground in the dip is damp, so I sit on my backpack. We could sleep on my tarp, but I won't suggest it because I'll creep back to the canal path as soon as she's asleep and put a few miles between us.

I hear her footsteps—they're quicker than I expect. In my mind, I see her with a rock in her hand. I leap up and twist around.

"What's the matter?" she asks.

"An animal. I thought I heard an animal."

She pulls two apples from her bag. "Fruit again," she says. After a mouthful, she adds, "You know, Caleb, finding the canal was the difficult part. We are free."

"And when we reach Wales . . . ?"

"We can join the seasonal workers, move from farm to farm, pick fruit."

"What happens when all the fruit has been picked?"

She shrugs her shoulders. "We'll work something out. Find an empty house. Grow our own food." Odette pulls on a hat. "I'm tired." She lies down and snuggles around her bag.

Odette's plan is shit.

I move as far as I dare from her and lie down with one arm through the strap of my backpack, like I did when I camped with Mother. What would she think of me? Mother had a real plan, one with simple goals: reach a reception centre, place our trust in the authorities, work for as long as the authorities dictated until we won the right to settle and make a new home. I should never have trusted Skylark. Trusting people like Skylark wasn't part of Mother's plan.

———

I'm woken by voices on the canal path. Idiot. I fell asleep. Still woozy, I stay still, waiting for the voices to fade. In a flash, it occurs to me:

Ma Lexie will have discovered the unlocked steel door. I imagine her running across the roof to my hut, flinging the door open. I hope she feels bad.

I pull myself to my feet. Odette doesn't move at all; she's a dumb rock. I pick my way as quietly as I can back to the canal and start walking. I check the position of the sun. It's midmorning. The people I heard on the canal path are now far off, walking north. I stride out. I'm smiling. I start to jog in case by some sixth sense Odette suddenly wakes. It's better she thinks I ran away as soon as she fell asleep.

The canal follows a gentle curve, and after a few minutes I turn around. Odette wouldn't see me now—the patch of woodland is way behind me. I drop my backpack and take the water bottle from the side pocket. Leaning my head back, I take a swig and feel the two keys move against my chest. I pull the ribbon up and over my head, and I stare at them. Yesterday the keys marked me out as Ma Lexie's new boy. Holding the knotted end of the ribbon, I swing the keys gently back and forth. With a flick of the wrist, I throw them in the canal.

I'm on my own. It feels good.

I look down at myself. I'd look better in shorts and T-shirt, so I quickly change. Then I jog some more. And as I do, I decide that I've made some bad decisions since Mother disappeared, but from today I'll stick to the plan. I'll have to find a police station, hand myself in. After all, I have my papers. I can prove who I am, that I'm younger than I look. At least the police will take me to a reception centre, and if I ask nicely they might even look for my parents.

I look over my shoulder again. In the distance, I see a barge heading down the canal in my direction. I stop and watch. As it nears, I see it's loaded with a heap of earth, with an upside-down wheelbarrow chucked on top. A man at the rudder is looking straight ahead, down the length of the barge, as if his thoughts are a million miles away. But as he approaches, I wave and smile. "Nice day, isn't it?" I call out.

He raises his eyebrows, woken from his daydream. He nods at me. The barge passes by, and he twists around.

"Want a lift?"

I shout back, "Not today, thank you."

I can be friendly, but I'm not trusting anyone again. I'll trust my own two feet.

CHAPTER 4

SKYLARK

ithin sixty seconds of her message hitting me, I'd jumped down the hostel stairwell three steps at a time and leapt on my bike, but I didn't tear up the streets because the sidecar's been rattling these last few days like it's full of empty cans, and I really must check it out before it frikkin' detaches, goes careering off and smashes. I took it slow, but I still made enough noise to wake the whole enclave. Ha! Can't be helped.

Ma Lexie's message struck her usual arse-y tone. *Get over here now!* Strictly business. She's not one for small talk. When I'm around her, I act real breezy in the hope she'll copycat because she's the type of woman who shows a nice-as-pie face to family and any fella she fancies, but with me and the rest of the world the shutters come down. I kinda wish she could loosen up. Sometimes, I think she'd like to be friends, but she holds back like she has a voice in her head saying, *Don't waste your time.*

That night I delivered Caleb to her—dead on my feet, cold, hungry, way beyond weary—she gave me no thanks for keeping him out of Jaspar's mitts, and he took some persuading. Ma Lexie quizzed me about the boy, his background, whether anyone would be searching for him. All the while, I prayed she'd offer me a hot meal, a bit of floor space to crash because, by then, the hostel had shut its doors for the night. But no, she offered no food, no floor space, and I doubt it even crossed her mind. Did she realise I'd be sleeping in a stairwell?

No idea what's lit her fuse this morning. She might have given me a clue. Maybe she's sick and flapping because it's market day, or the boys are sick. Anyway, what's any of that to me? If she doesn't want me as a friend, she can't expect favours.

I take the first flight up her stairwell two steps at a time, slowing to a trudge at the top-floor landing, where I hear voices, not from her flat but from the roof. Oh God. Sounds like Jaspar.

Stepping out onto the roof through the open access door, I spot the two of them beyond the solar arrays by the overseer's hut, so I call out, "I can hear you from the ground floor." Slight exaggeration.

"Shut the fucken door, then," shouts Jaspar.

I clang it closed, noisier than necessary, and head over to them. A family standoff from the looks of it, and I guess I'm being dragged into it. Ma Lexie is shrinking into herself. Her head is dipped, and she holds her fist to her mouth. Jaspar strides away from her, stops and swivels, stabs a finger towards her, opens his mouth but doesn't speak. Instead, he walks right up to her. She looks up into his face, and he stoops, his nose almost touching hers, and I bet he's going cross-eyed trying to focus on her that close. I walk through the arrays, stopping some distance away as if in deference—giving them *quality family time*.

He snaps, "Not happy. Not happy at all." Like he's repeating a tough-guy line from a movie, which makes him ridiculous, laughable. He should hear himself.

He turns to me and says, "The kids have all fucken scarpered."

I twist around, looking across the roof.

He calls across: "Don't you fucken believe me?" He turns back to Lexie. "I could've put them lads to work at the yard. And you go all soft and give that kid a sodding key."

I'm cringing. Oh shit, Ma Lexie. What's he going to do? He's mad enough to punch her, and she needs to brace herself, but instead she's staring up at the sky as if she's given up, as if she doesn't care if a smack's coming her way. I jump in because I can't stand Jaspar, the witless wonder, and I wouldn't like to be on the receiving end. "They won't get far, Jaspar. They're only kids. I'll put the word out. And you should—"

"Shut it! Don't tell *me* what to do, you with them stupid feathers. I've got people on it. Right?"

Ma Lexie backs away from him, then edges towards me. "Skylark's right, Jasp. They'll have no idea where to go. And I'm sorry, it won't—"

"Too late for that. You never learn, do you, Lex? Warned you before, haven't I? Eh? Don't get soft. Don't get mumsy."

She nods and hugs herself as if she's caught outdoors wearing a thin dress on a freezing cold day. She's shrinking right in front of my eyes. Christ, Lexie, you need to stand up to Jasp because that's the way you deal with a bully like him. Tell him. Tell him there's nothing special about those three lads. Plenty more where they came from.

I can't believe Caleb could be so dim. Two small kids will slow him down, and it's far easier to spot a threesome on the run. And none of this would have happened if Ma Lexie hadn't been pissing about yesterday, sending Caleb on a walkabout. Bet she hasn't fessed up to Jaspar about that, about hitting the kid. What a mess.

I count to five in my head to try and calm myself, because today was supposed to be my lazy day before going back on the road. Jaspar kicks the shed door closed. It bounces back. I suppose he wanted a quiet Sunday morning too, especially as he's had a late night, judging by his bloodshot eyes.

"What about your local police pals?" I ask.

"Yeah, I've covered that. I'll hear if they've picked them up." He turns his head and spits. "It pisses me off to have this fucken hassle. If we get them back, Lex, they're working for me from now on. You'll have to manage on your own. Do your own sewing and stuff."

There's a hell of a banging across the street, so I glance over but can't see any movement on the rooftop garden. I look back at Jaspar, who starts off on Lexie again. "Why should I help you out when you're doing your best to—?"

We all stare across at the next block, at the roof garden. Someone's pounding on the access door from the stairwell, and it sounds like they're whacking the metal door with a hammer. Muffled shouting, but I can't make out what they're saying. More hammering and Jaspar, hands on hips, explodes: "What's the bloody racket over there?"

Ma Lexie, no doubt glad of the interruption, walks across to the parapet wall, leans over and shouts, "Mr. Entwistle!" She waits and calls again. I join her at the railing. His face appears at the top-floor window. "Up here, Mr. Entwistle. What's going on?" she calls.

"The janitor's gone missing. The door to her flat is unlocked. And her girl's not opening the roof door."

"Someone must have a spare key."

Mr. Entwistle shouts back: "Her daughter has one. She's on her way but someone's getting impatient up there."

She throws him a thank-you wave and turns back to face more music from Jaspar.

"Find your own labourers, got it, Lex?" he says. "I found you a nice flat and wangled the janitor's job. As far as I see it, I've done enough. I don't want all this stupid add-on stress."

Not that I owe her anything either, but I decide to do her thinking for her. She's punch-drunk. "Lexie can deal direct with me for her labour from now on, Jaspar. Not a problem. But can she still have free recyclables from the yard?" He nods. That was easy, so I ask for more. "Can she still use your safe?"

He throws his head back. "I'll think about it. I'll talk to the family. But, to tell you the truth, Lex, it's about time you stopped leaning on us."

She comes to her senses at long last. "It's true, Jasp. You've all been kind since Ruben . . . I know you don't owe me. I messed up with the kids, but that won't happen again. I need this business. Don't know what I'd—"

"All right. All right!"

Ha. I should be a politician. No, a diplomat. That's it. In my line of work I know about persuasion and calming people down. "Come on, Lexie," I say and take her arm. "Business as usual. I'll give you a hand setting up the stall. You're running late already."

Jaspar rolls back his shoulders as though purging acid from his muscles. "Both of you." He stabs at each of us with that mean finger of his. "Come to the yard when the market closes. We need to talk. And Skylark, if you hear anything about our little band of brothers, tell me, soon as."

With that, the three of us head off towards Ma Lexie's work shed, and as we take our separate paths through the solar arrays, the neighbour's roof door swings outward. Three people step out onto the roof, fan out and start calling for Odette. And, as we reach the work shed, a man's voice, loud and clear: "Oh my God!" We all swivel around to see him emerge from a small shed. "She's dead!"

"What the hell?" says Jaspar. He grabs each of us by the arm and pushes us into the work shed.

"Let go, Jasp. I'll find out what's happening," says Lexie. She hurries across the roof, leans over the parapet and calls to Mr. Entwistle. She waits half a minute and calls again. My mind's doing frikkin' somersaults. The girl's dead? The janitor's missing. What's going on? Has the janitor murdered the girl? If she has, why would she bother running off? The girl's bound to be undocumented.

Mr. Entwistle reappears at his window and shouts up to Lexie. "The janitor's dead! Blood everywhere."

"The *janitor*? Where's the girl?" calls Lexie.

"No sign of her. Gone."

Jaspar and I are rooted to the spot. Ma Lexie returns to the work shed. She says, almost to herself, "The boys are gone. The girl is gone . . ." She looks at me, focusing. "I've seen Caleb wave to her. Told him not to."

I'm trying to make sense of it all, thinking aloud. "So . . . as soon as Caleb got the key . . . the girl murders her boss, and they all run off. *Four* kids on the run. And one of them's a murderer."

Jaspar isn't listening. He's ahead of us. His frown lines tell me he's already working out what to do. He isn't angry when he speaks to Lexie. Just cold. "Listen and do as I say." His voice is flat, matter-of-fact. "Don't tell anyone our boys are gone. Go now, set up the stall, Lex. If anyone asks why Caleb isn't with you, tell them the kid works for me. Yesterday was a one-off. Yeah?"

Boy, he spins a story right quick. Ma Lexie nods, grabs the trolley and turns to me. "Carry the clothes boxes down the stairs for me."

Jaspar cuts in. "As soon as you've done that, get back here, Skylark. Lexie can set up the stall on her own."

"Tell me what to do," I say.

"Get rid of any sign of them three kids," says Jaspar. "Their bedding, their chairs, plates, clothes, everything. The police—if they can be arsed with an enclave murder—will be over here asking if Lexie saw anything from this roof, heard any noise last night, any argument. We don't want them guessing we've had workers up here with no papers. And God knows we don't want them guessing our kids did a runner too. As long as they're looking for a runaway girl, a girl on her own, they're not likely to find her or any of them. If they do, we'll be in the fucken firing line."

Ma Lexie's trying to gather her stuff, her feet doing a quickstep, like she's trying to go in three directions at once. She stops. "Jasp. Could be a coincidence. Don't you think? The girl might have run off on her own."

"They're all in it together. Obvious! Thing is, the police could be here soon, and they'll be poking around. So, I'm off."

Which makes sense. He might be related to Ma Lexie, but he'd have difficulty explaining why he's here early on a Sunday morning.

———

I've cleared the easy stuff and shifted all the dishes and chairs to Ma Lexie's flat. If the police wheedle their way into her place, I guess they'll notice the excess of chairs. She'll have to move them out of the block later, but at least they're off the roof. And I've dumped the kids' spare clothes—not many of those—on the pile of recycled materials, plus I've stuffed their bedding in my sidecar. But Caleb's mattress in the overseer's hut is a problem. I message Jaspar, ask him what I should do with it, and he tells me to drop it off the back of the roof in fifteen minutes, and he'll have a lad with a trailer waiting below to fetch it to the yard.

Mustn't hang around myself. I don't want any cosy chats with the police, so I make a final check across the roof, through the work shed, picking up a pair of small flip-flops that I'd missed earlier, and finally drag out the manky mattress from the shed. I notice a bunch of papers, rolled up, and after I've pulled the mattress over to the parapet wall, I go back to pick them up. I don't want to linger, so I push the papers into my pocket. I rush back to the parapet and look down the building to see where the window shutters are neatly pushed back, and I pick the best spot to throw over the mattress. Don't want to cause any damage, draw any attention, or risk a complaint.

A few minutes earlier than Jaspar instructed, checking there's no one walking along the street, I shove the mattress over the railing.

———

Ma Lexie may have lost her kids, but what do I care? It's all extra business for me—repeat business—which is the best kind in my book. I'm always nervous about taking on a new client because you never know if you're getting snared in some sting operation by immigration officers. I've made good money these past three years from Jaspar's operations and from a handful of farms, but this morning's drama has got me thinking again that this a high-risk business, and I shouldn't forget that, even when everything seems fine and dandy. I'm beginning to think I should quit while I'm ahead, apply for an enclave flat, go back to my old business: simple courier work, nothing dodgy. I mean, I fell into this work—a chance conversation with a woman in a Liverpool pub, and I agreed to take one lad over to a recycling yard, Jaspar's as it turned out. And that Liverpool contact kept me busy for weeks on twice my usual pay delivering one migrant after another. Then this same contact asked me to help out over in France near the coast, and the money she offered was way too good to turn down. I've a decent stash of savings now, so I reckon that all my hard work and discomforts have been worth it.

No sign of the police when I step out into the street, so I head off, without glancing backwards, to my favourite hangout in the enclave: a coffee shop on the ground floor of a block of flats—one of the first blocks to be built here. The flats were bigger at the beginning, even had their own showers and toilets. In each flat. Since then, the housing department's turned proper stingy. No flats are built now with their own toilets and showers. Shared toilets in each block, and showers in alternate blocks. Lucky for me, the hostels have both.

It strikes me, walking to the coffee shop, that I should decide what's best for *me*. Stop chasing around for the likes of Jaspar and Ma Lexie.

The door to the coffee shop is no different from any door in any block of flats. There's no sign up or anything because the coffee shop doesn't have a business permit. Funny. A speakeasy for coffee drinkers, run by two brothers who rent neighbouring flats. They persuaded the authorities they needed a connecting door because of the older brother's care needs. A ruse most likely, with some official paid off in the housing department to push it through. That's the kind of job everyone wants: a small but reliable wage in a local government office with the opportunity for a few tips. Nothing exorbitant or even obligatory. Enough to cover a meal out once in a while, put something aside for retirement, small treats that the wage can't cover. Anyway, that's the way the world works when wages are low. Everyone knows that.

I tap the door, see the spy hole darken, and the door opens. Classical music is playing as usual—less likely to attract complaints from the neighbours—and I drop into one of three battered but comfy sofas positioned around a long coffee table. A middle-aged woman is sitting across from me, knitting. She looks up for the briefest moment, flicker of a smile, and returns to her clickety-clacking.

The younger brother, Carlo, appears from the adjoining flat. "The usual? Black coffee?" he asks.

"Yeah, thanks. Too late for breakfast?"

"No. Cold or hot?"

"Cold, please."

I mean, this is all I've needed since I ran away from home—a few comfy haunts, a string of safe bars and coffeehouses, the familiar face of a server. That's been enough. For me it's been safer to keep away from legit hangouts. I prefer a fleapit like this where I feel welcome and no one asks those awkward questions like: Where are you from? What's your line of work? And mostly I don't care where I sleep. Hostels have been fine. I've promised myself that when I get my own flat, whenever, I won't accumulate crap like most people do. I'll keep it simple.

I remember the roll of paper I picked up in Caleb's hut. I dig it out from a deep pocket in my shorts, untie the frayed strip of fabric that binds the roll and flatten the papers on the table. They're scraps, bits of packaging, seed packets—why would Caleb have old seed packets—and faint handwriting on each one, in block capitals. It's dark in my corner of room, so I angle a seed packet towards the window. God, I really need to sort out my eyesight. I fancy some old-fashioned spectacles, but the retro look might make me too noticeable. For that matter, this jacket with the feathered collar is too distinct. I put the seed packet down. I mean, someone might drop my name, or mention that some woman with a feathered jacket brings kids to Jaspar's yard and has furtive conversations with the boss.

I'll ditch the jacket. In any case, the feathers look raggedy. I should have thrown it away after the moth infestation—lots of teeny-tiny moths. Instead, I fixed the problem by holding the jacket over a smoking open fire. That did the trick, but it's not been the same since.

I look back at the seed packet, flip it over—marigolds—and flip it back over. The writing is in pencil, and I can't make anything out in this light.

Carlo sets my breakfast down, taking care that the coffee doesn't slop over the side of the mug. Always fills it to the top. I like that.

I know why I've held on to my jacket. It's the one thing I've managed to make with my own two hands since I hit the road. There's not much opportunity and I miss my hobbies. I kinda envy Ma Lexie and her clothing business. Still, I'm better off away from home, away from my parents' poxy flat, almost stripped bare, in one of the poxiest Nottingham enclaves.

I slurp the hot coffee and bite into Carlo's famous cheese roll with curried pickle. Nice. Feel much better and I find myself smiling, not so much about the grub, but about My Great Escape. My dad must have hit the frikkin' roof. The woman opposite catches me smiling. I stole his precious bike and sidecar. He was going to sell it anyway, like he sold the fridge, for Christ's sake. He'd have sold the bike cheap and wasted the money within days, splashing out on new clothes and fancy food, pretending he was some heavy dude. I hated him flashing his credits at me when he sold the tall mirror—saying no one needs to see their feet. Hardly a stick of furniture left in the house. Serves him right. I mean, if I'd had the benefit of proper parenting, I would never have stolen anything.

I stand and shuffle across to the window to take a closer look at the marigold packet and the pencilled handwriting.

In the markit, find me a small torch. Throw it to me tonite. Do not miss.

Oh, Christ on a bike! I gawp at the tatty paper with its faded symbols—when to sow, how deep to sow.

What's going on? The girl threw a message to Caleb? She sent him on an errand? Jeez, he's in this up to his neck. And he lied to us. I mean, I actually believed the little bugger. He *did* give me the slip in the market. Did he find a torch for her? And what's this next message?

Clever boy. Bring me a prez from the markit.

Next one: *Wats goin on your roof. I seen no fat man tday.*

These must be going back in time. I'm peeling them back:

Old bitch wake me early agin. to much to do.

To hot. Ask boss if I can stand in shady. No.

Herd you all laffing last nite. I have no one to laff with.

What's going on here? I flip through them. All pretty boring but there's so many, and from time to time there's a creepy message like this one: *I like your dark hair. Like a boy back home.*

Did the girl start this? I bet she frikkin' did. I flip through the scraps of paper again, shaking my head. I reckon she's groomed him—the bitch—right under Ma Lexie's nose.

———

Feeling almost chilly because I've dumped my leather jacket, feathers and all. It hasn't been off my back in two years. I'm used to wearing lots of layers even on a scorching hot day. It cuts down on the packing if I wear more, and it's become normal to *overdress*. I have one small backpack, that's all, because I need all the space in the sidecar for a passenger and their baggage. And I guess I smell better now, because that leather jacket absorbed a lot of grief since I shifted my courier work into the people-carrying business. It's a sweatier line of work, takes me into less salubrious settings, if you will. Encampments by the road, shanties in the sand dunes, shack cities under flyovers, squats in old deserted docklands. The worst are those desperate camps deep in forests where people have pretty much given up on the real world. No matter what I offer these forest folk—regular work with accommodation, seasonal jobs on a farm—they don't want to know. They simply don't *get* regular life any longer. They'd rather spend half the day fetching water from dirty streams than do any actual work. So I tend to stay away from those hardcore dropouts. They can't *reassimilate*. Forgotten all their house training.

On the upside, I do get to spend time with some interesting people, and I've never met anyone out on the road who hasn't a story to tell. I like to get people talking. I like to think I'm doing my bit to help people make a fresh start, rescuing them from a bad situation and taking them to a less bad situation. Though they'll have a tough time reaching their full potential with the likes of Jaspar as a boss. Ma Lexie is another matter entirely, but she went too far in the opposite direction. She was way too quick to promote young Caleb.

I try to imagine Ma Lexie when her Ruben was still alive. I never met the fella, but the clear impression I've gathered on the street is that Ruben wasn't the sharpest knife in the drawer. That's probably a gob-shite thing to even think, given the nature of his sudden ending. Maybe for Lexie the attraction of Ruben was all chemistry, and there's nothing wrong with that. And she didn't just marry Ruben—she married into the business. What a leg-up. But, if she doesn't sharpen up—jeez, stop thinking about *sharp, knives, etcetera*—she'll end up with nothing. Doesn't she know you don't get lucky twice? I mean, she's shown everyone she has real get-up-and-go, the beginnings of a good business, but she'll chuck it all away if she doesn't toughen up.

I've never had any connections to help me out—no quality business contacts aka legitimate ones and no family connections. No parent-as-flippin'-mentor. A feckless father and a hypochondriac for a mother who hadn't done a stroke of work in God knows how many years. Self-absorbed, self-pitying. Complete waste of space, all my family. Could

I make a success of myself without having to break the goddamn law? Is this the right time to start afresh? Before another cock-up. What if Caleb gets arrested by immigration, and he starts talking about me, how I found him, where I took him?

―――

This is the last time, I promise myself. My last visit to the recycling yard, last meeting with Jaspar and any of his clan. I should have quit sooner, but it's easier to carry on doing what you did yesterday. You know the ropes and the money's good. It's not easy money, but I've found my own methods, my own way of making the job a smooth operation. Take Caleb. Pretty much a stray cat when I came across him. He barely spoke to me when I first sat down with him, but he kept sneaking a look at my bike and sidecar. I knew I'd get through to him eventually. With quiet nervous kids like him, in need of help, I do all the talking until I find something that lights a little spark in them, and usually it's their pets. Do you have a pet at home? What's its name? That kind of thing gets them talking, because I've noticed that they miss their pets as much as their families. But with Caleb, I promised him a ride on the bike. Then slowly he started to open up, talked about his mum, as though their separation was temporary, as though she'd been distracted by an errand in town, and they'd meet up later. He said he'd find her again if he headed to Manchester, because that's where they were headed in the first place, and all he'd have to do is find their compatriots who had already left their town and settled in that city. I remember he looked at me properly, in the eyes, for the first time and said, "It shouldn't be too difficult. We'll find one another there."

All the time we sat together—me coaxing, and him listening, sometimes talking—he pulled and nipped the left side of his neck. A red raw patch of skin below his ear. I told him, he'd get infected if he carried on. And while I cleaned the wound, I learned, little by little, that he didn't have an address in Manchester, or the name of a particular person. If I'd been his parent, I'd have made sure we had a fail-safe meeting point, a name, an address, if only the name of a shop or a bar owned by someone from their community, or at least spoke their language, who could put out a call for them. I mean, it's not my job to give him the wake-up call, and I didn't dampen his hopes. Didn't explain that any plans he might have should be seen as long-term. He was awful thin and dirty. I knew if I gave him to Ma Lexie she would build up his strength. When he was stronger, older, he could go looking for his mum and dad.

There's no one coming or going in the yard when I park my bike. The recycling conveyors never stop, and the ruckus is like background music you can't shut out, or like a rookery in spring when the birds never stop squawking. But at least the sound of the conveyors is the sound of money being made.

I knock on Jaspar's container office and step in. Jaspar and Ma Lexie stand with their backs to me, side by side. Through their legs I can see two chairs and two pairs of small feet, toes just touching the floor. Lexie turns around, and I catch sight of the kids—Zach and Mikey.

"They're okay," says Ma Lexie.

"Who found them?" I ask.

"Some old fella, a night guard down by the workshops," says Ma Lexie. "Saw them sneaking around. Told his mate Frankie, who has clan connections. Frankie put the word out."

"No damage done, then?" I ask.

"No police involved, if that's what you mean," says Jaspar. "Not yet anyway. Depends on the other fucker, Caleb, if he gets nabbed with the girl in tow."

I step forward and see the kids, slumped, and I feel sorry for them. "Hey, boys. What happened to Caleb?" I crouch down and take Mikey's hand. "Did he walk too fast? You couldn't keep up with him, Mikey?"

The kid looks up at Jaspar, and it's Jaspar who tells the story. Seems Mikey heard a noise on the roof last night and was scared. He woke

Zach, who went to look around and found the roof access door open. They hunted for Caleb but couldn't find him, and he wasn't in his hut. They decided to run off too.

"They don't know anything about Caleb or the girl. They didn't all leave together," says Ma Lexie.

"Listen," I say to Zach. "Did Caleb have a girlfriend? The girl on the roof garden next door?"

Jaspar answers for him. "They saw him wave to her now and then."

This is the moment when I should mention the messages on the frikkin' seed packets, but why should I bother? I can't see how these messages will help. They'll only confirm that Caleb and the girl were friends and she was, most likely, hatching some sort of plan. No, I'll keep my mouth shut. I've already done them a big favour, clearing the roof. I could easily have been spotted. I mean, runaways are definitely peripheral to my business. Runaways are other people's problem.

I pretend that I'm eager to find out more. "Zach, did he ever call across to her?"

"We've gone through all that," says Jaspar.

I persist. "You see, Zach, that girl has run away too, and she could get Caleb into a ton of trouble."

Zach wipes away tears. "I don't care."

I twist around and catch Ma Lexie's eye. "Did the police come to you today, at the stall?"

She shakes her head.

"One of my crew's keeping a lookout," says Jaspar. "He says the police still haven't taken the body away. No one's been into Lexie's building. Yet."

I'm pretty damn keen to make my exit because Jaspar needs to make a decision, namely where to billet the kids, and I don't want to get involved. They can't go back with Lexie, at least not until the whole thing's died down, and that could take weeks unless the police decide they couldn't care less. Even then, Jaspar might refuse to let Ma Lexie have the kids back. He might follow through with his threat and make her work on her own.

"Look. The police will be doing the bare minimum, Jaspar," I say. "They'll send out a few drones looking for the girl. But I bet they've no data on her. She's probably an illegal. I expect they're working on vague descriptions of her by the garden visitors. And there'll be no trace of her in the janitor's flat, no documentation."

Ma Lexie speaks up at last. "The police have no idea she's on the run with a boy. Or might—"

Jaspar cuts her off. "I've had a belly full of this. I'll keep the kids here in the warehouse dorm. I'll ask the family later if anyone can make use of them."

Ma Lexie goes all quiet again. I know what's going on in her head. She thinks of herself as a good person, but when the chips are down, she's a survivor like everyone else around here. She isn't going to plead for those kids even though we both know the dorm here is a tough place for any illegal, let alone a couple of youngsters.

"Let me know if I can help, Ma Lexie," I say without too much enthusiasm. I slip away and cross the yard, feeling bad that I didn't wave or say anything to Zach and Mikey as I left. I poke around in the piles of textiles in the warehouse. Find myself a shapeless jacket, one my mother would wear. Blue, bland, altogether forgettable.

Before I leave the yard, I borrow some tools from a guy repairing a trailer. I need to tighten up the sidecar fixings. The last thing I want to see is my sidecar in a ditch. If I can fix it here, I can head out in the morning at first light, put some distance between me and the clan and the whole frikkin' mess with Caleb and the girl. Then what? Pack in this business? Or, finish the season first? Right now, it's early harvest, and I supply three vineyards that still handpick. Not that I've met the farmers. I've never set foot on a vineyard. I meet the fixers, and I doubt they've ever seen a bunch of grapes on the vine.

I try a few spanners until I find the right size. Lying on my side, I tighten each nut in turn across the undercarriage. One is gunked up with mud and grit and it won't budge. I wipe the surface of the nut and spray some oil, cadged from the mechanic, and wait for it to penetrate and loosen everything up.

That Caleb is either smarter or more stupid than I first realised, and I can't make up my mind which it is. He's at the age where he could be both—brainy and thick at the same time. He probably made a dash for it without weighing up the risks. I reckon the whole thing was a knee-jerk, what with Ma Lexie losing her rag at him. He decided on instinct, and he's probably regretting his decision already. Probably living rough under some hedgerow like his mum. Is this how it goes? Like if these illegals don't settle to their fate—and let's face it, Caleb landed on his feet with Ma Lexie, compared with most alternatives—they end up sliding into more and more chaos. It doesn't make sense. I mean, warm bed on a roof versus damp hedgerows, waking up surrounded by fields covered in dew, a cow mooing in your frikkin' face. What the hell has he gained?

———

Out on the road, I focus on the ride, the potholes. I have to concentrate but I'm right happy. I love the start of a new journey. It's the best feeling in the world, mounting the bike, and I've felt the same thrill ever since I sped off from home in the middle of the night. About a month after I'd left, I got in touch with a good mate in our block, and he told me my dad didn't report his bike as stolen. Kinda proud about that, and I half suspect, but this could be a flight of fancy, that he's even a little proud of me having the gumption to do it. In his own day, he was Jack the Lad by all accounts. He must like it, just a bit, that I've got his genes and not my mum's.

Someone's trying to message me, so I pull over on a stretch of road shaded by trees. It's Ma Lexie, and I can't hardly believe my eyes when I read her message: *Thanks for yesterday, Skylark. Fighting my corner with Jasp like you did, and clearing up too. See you soon. Lex.*

Three whole sentences. I mean, could this be the start of a beautiful new friendship?

PART 2

CHAPTER 5

CALEB

The runner, Jerome, reaches my picking spot along the row of vines, and I tip my full-to-the-very-top basket of green grapes into his hod.

"Good work," he says.

He's the one runner who speaks to me. I untie the knee pads that hang from a belt loop on my shorts and strap them on. Kneeling is the easiest way for me, but I can't do a full day in one picking position. You have to mix it up.

That's the big lesson I learned when I started here. I worked for three days bending over to do all my cutting. I ached all over. My right hand and arm were burning from gripping and squeezing the secateurs. The pain was as bad as the time my thigh was knifed.

Now, after three weeks as a picker, I've found the right way. If I change my position every hour, my back is only half-broken at the end of the day. I spend one hour—or what feels like one hour—standing up, bending over to cut each bunch of grapes from the vine, then one hour on my knees, then one hour moving along the row on my bum, which isn't the fastest way of picking. I'm getting stronger, building the grape-picker's muscles in my back, across my shoulders and along my arms.

This is much, much harder work than unpicking and sewing at Ma Lexie's. But, if I don't count the first few days on the vineyard, I've been happier. It's better working in the countryside than on Ma Lexie's roof. And I've stopped stressing, because I heard the supervisor say he didn't need any more hands. So, I'm no longer looking over my shoulder every five minutes to see if Odette has turned up. I've no idea what I'd say to her. I keep telling myself to stop sweating. She was heading for Wales. I've stayed on the English side of the border, in a place called Shropshire.

I'm glad to be kneeling again.

I hear the supervisor shouting for the runners to speed up. I got on his wrong side for the first few days. He'd call my name and I'd ignore him, forgetting I'd given a false name when I arrived. I'm calling myself Leo—my best friend's name back home—because someone might come looking for a runaway named Caleb. Quick thinking on my part. The supervisor here isn't too bad, better than that bastard Mr. Ben at Ma Lexie's. And the food's better, and there's more of it. My best days are like today when Jerome is the runner on my row. He's the only runner who remembers to bring us water between breaks. On bad days, I eat a few grapes if I get thirsty. It's the runners' job to bring us water, but they always make excuses: it's nearly break time, or they'll bring it next time, which they don't. I hate them.

When I left Odette by the canal side, I kept changing my mind— should I head for the farms and vineyards, or should I hand myself in to the authorities? Finding a police station or even a police officer sounds easy, but it isn't in the countryside. This is all I saw: canal paths, hedges, fields and a few houses in the distance. I decided to head for the farms and vineyards. I liked the fresh air too much to give it up. From then on, I hid during the day, walked at night. What worried me was the thought that I'd be nabbed again, not by Skylark but by someone like her pretending to be kind, and then finding myself trapped someplace even worse than the roof, or Jaspar's recycling yard.

The whistle blows for break time sooner than I expect, which must mean I'm getting better at the job. I walk uphill along the row to the dirt track, and I hear the farmer's drone whizzing over my head. I hope it's carrying some chocolate today. We get twenty minutes. It's just enough time to eat some bread and cheese, and glug as much water as I can. I never need to pee during the day, so I know I'm not drinking enough. Some of the workers drink wine, but I avoid it, hate the taste. At lunchtime when we all sit out by the vineyard track, I do take a swig of wine to make them all think I'm older than I am.

I reach the track, and the supervisor is already unloading the drone's basket and passing out bread, meats, tomatoes, cheeses. And, yes, there's a few chocolate bars. Can't be bad.

"Where's Eleanor?" asks Maria, one of the local workers. "She must be going deaf."

The supervisor is biting on a chunk of bread. He points at me. "Leo!" Crumbs drop down his chest. "Go and look for her. Fourth or fifth row."

"But—"

"Go on. Do it!"

Why should I miss part of my break? Hope he chokes. He should go and find her himself. He does next to nothing, spends all day walking backwards and forwards checking on us.

When he blows his whistle for the end of break, I won't rush back to work. I've earned my twenty minutes. I head towards the fourth row, but Maria calls out, "Not that one. The other side of the red roses."

When I first came here, I thought the roses were planted to make the place look prettier. I was wrong. They're planted to bring bees to the rows of vines, but it sounds like a superstition to me.

I can't see Eleanor. The rows are long and slope downhill. I think Maria told me the wrong row. I jump up to peek over the top of the vines, hoping to catch sight of her. But if she's picking she'll be stooped, and she's short anyway. I crouch down and peer through the rows. Nothing. I jog downhill. A crow squawks and I pull up. Not because of the squawk. I've seen a red bundle on the ground. Eleanor wears red.

I run and kneel down next to her. She lies on her side, facing away from me. Bending over her, I shake her arm. She's wheezing real bad.

I jump up and wave and shout, "Come quick." And then holler, "Hey! Come quick." Eleanor's face is purple. A silver chain around her neck has snapped, and a locket has fallen to the ground. I look over my shoulder. No one in the row yet. I lift her head and slide off the chain, drop it into a crack in the ground. Look over my shoulder again as Maria turns into the row. I lay my hand over the locket, pick it up and slide it into my pocket as I stand up. "Hurry," I shout, "She's bad!"

———

I don't think we'll be picking any more grapes this morning. The supervisor called an ambulance straightaway, and within two minutes some of the seasonal pickers had disappeared. I heard one of them say that when there's an ambulance you can expect the police to visit next. I knew that meant difficult questions: Where's your work permit? Where's your return ticket home?

I hang around Eleanor's workmates, the other local men and women. No one tries to lift Eleanor, but Maria has already rolled her onto her left side, and she's wiping Eleanor's face and arms with a wet cloth, trying to cool her down. I walk over to the supervisor and ask if I need to stay as I was the one who found her. He doesn't even look at me. "Make yourself scarce, kid."

Eleanor is a local woman, so they have to get medical help. They have no choice.

I didn't speak to her much, but one time she asked me how old I was. When I told her, trying to sound convincing, that I was eighteen, she said, "That's a shame." What did she mean? I didn't like to ask. I guess she meant it's a shame I have to work so hard at my age. Makes me think. I wish I was back home and eighteen years old already, because I could finish school and get a job. But my parents probably wouldn't allow that to happen. It's my father; he's the one who'd make me keep on studying. Would my mother try to persuade him? No, I think she'd take sides with him.

And now, here I am, sweating, thirsty, doing a job that any idiot can do. The skin on my nose has burnt and actually scabbed. Maybe I was stupid running away from Ma Lexie. She gave me a real chance, wanted to give me my own label. There will never *ever* be a wine bottle with a Caleb label. I kick a clod of earth. Why don't you know when you're making a real bad decision?

I climb back up to the track, grab a hunk of bread and cheese, swat the flies. I stuff my pockets with the chocolate and a tin of sardines, which was meant for Eleanor. She won't need it now. I drink more water and set off. There's about ten of us travelling seasonal workers— I'm not sure who's legal and who's illegal—and we camp out in a flat field about twenty minutes' walk away from this particular field. The owner of the vineyard loaned me an old tent and sleeping bag—didn't ask where I came from. Some of the seasonal workers bring their own camping gear, and they're totally organised with folding chairs and solar cookers. But I manage fine with the free food we get from the owner.

The one good thing about this vineyard, apart from the fresh air and the food, is the locker room, which is hidden from view in an old barn. There's one locker for each worker. I don't have to worry about my stuff being stolen. And whenever I see any tinned food lying around, going spare, I pick it up and store it in my locker. If I ever need to do another runner, I'll be better prepared than last time.

It's weird, walking in the countryside on my own like this. Out of sight from the field we're harvesting, and out of sight of the camping ground. Normally, I'd be walking with all the other workers, keeping myself to myself, pretending I don't notice things. Like the bald French man who thinks he can tease the young French woman just because they're from the same country, like that makes them a couple. He's an idiot. He can see she's not interested, but he isn't put off. Yesterday he grabbed her around her waist, in front of everyone. She totally lost it, shouted right in his face and threw punches. None of them landed. He laughed. Two of the other men pulled him away, but all the time they laughed and hooted, like the whole thing was one huge joke. The big guy, Jerome—who keeps to himself like I do—he strolled across and took a handful of the idiot's T-shirt and shoved him off the path. They all shut up then.

———

I hear scratching sounds near my tent. Rats, I guess. But there's nothing for them here. I never sneak any food into my tent, because the rats can smell it. They'd try to get in. Anyway, that's one of the rules: no food in the tents, and no lighting campfires.

My tent is yellow, a bit grubby, but I like it because I fall asleep knowing that, even if I have nightmares about Odette or Jaspar, or putting up tents, or fighting in deep mud, I'll wake up in a yellow light, and that tells me I'm safe. I don't keep much stuff with me—a warm top in case it gets cold in the night and a towel. Plus some toothpaste and a toothbrush, which I bought from the workers' shop. It's not a proper shop. Just a room in an outbuilding at the farmhouse. It's open for an hour at the end of the afternoon, and we can buy the basics there. It means I don't need to walk into the village. I don't dare to leave the vineyard.

So, so tired. I keep thinking about Eleanor, and it's stopping me from dropping off to sleep. She didn't need the locket. She has a home and her family. She'd forgive me if she understood. Like my mother said, you sometimes need to bribe your way when you're on the road. When you've spent all your money, you need to do a swap.

When I left Odette, I didn't have anything on me except one stupid orange. I got lucky though. During the second night's walk, heading south along the canal cutting through Shropshire, I came across a bar. It's called a pub here. No one around. I checked the bins at the back of the building and found half a pizza that was pretty clean, and some bits of bread that were dry. That saved me. Then on the third day in the late afternoon I came out of my daytime hideout—a patch of woodland as usual—and walked until I met a road bridge. I climbed up the embankment, and I saw some houses a short distance away along the country road. I decided to chance it, straightened my clothes, walked down into the village. I passed three or four people but kept my eyes down. I came to a small shop and looked at the notices in the window, hoping to get a clue about where I was. A girl came out of the shop and stopped. I could tell she was looking at me, but I didn't look back. She asked what I was looking for. Before I could say anything, she said, "That's my notice." She pointed at it. "I'm selling my blades. There, see? Black blades." I told her I wanted a fruit picker's job. She said, "Rather you than me. It's killing." I tried to ignore her, pretended to read the notices carefully. Then she said, "I saw a sign just outside the village at the Bowens' place. You know it?" I shook my head, and she pointed to a side road, told me they wanted pickers. "Up there. It's in full swing, you know. The first harvest. You're a bit late."

I thanked her and set off.

———

We start harvesting a new field today, the Rondo grapes for red wine. Our last day in the Phoenix field—the one where Eleanor fell ill—felt strange, embarrassing. After our morning break, Eleanor's daughter came to see the spot where her mother had collapsed, and she asked if anyone had seen her mother's locket and chain, that her mother must have lost it—a family keepsake—somewhere between the field and the ambulance. She was upset and asked everyone to help her in the search, which we did. After a few minutes, I held up the silver chain, as if I'd found it by chance. I didn't make a big deal of finding it. I asked Eleanor's daughter, "Is this it?" She chased over to me and began digging her fingers in the soil, desperate to find the actual locket. I'd already stashed it in my locker.

The pickers searched in the area where I found the chain and also along the path to where the ambulance had parked. The supervisor kept his mouth shut. Didn't tell us to get back to work. After fifteen minutes we gave up, but Eleanor's daughter stayed for ages turning over clods of soil.

———

All the itinerants, as they sometimes call us, are already picking Rondo grapes when the transport arrives, bringing the local workers from surrounding villages and small towns. They're late. I wait for the inevitable—shouts and complaints from the supervisor. But it's the locals' voices I hear. I wouldn't bother to get up if I was in my kneeling or sitting position. I'm doing my standing stoop, so I straighten up and look over the top of the vines to see what's going on. The locals are all in a huddle like a mob, facing the supervisor, and Maria's losing her temper, swinging her fists at the air—she doesn't have the nerve to hit him. Lots of finger jabbing, too, from the other locals.

Heads pop up along the rows of vines. Curious, like me, Jerome walks up to the track and stands with his hands on his hips a few paces away from the supervisor. As he walks back down the row of vines to his picking position, Jerome calls out so we can all hear him. He tells us the news that Eleanor died in hospital last night.

I bend down and carry on picking. I didn't know she'd die. I stole from a dead woman. Her daughter . . . the locket should be hers. It's too late to make it magically reappear. We're working in a different field now, and in any case, I opened the locket and threw away the photo inside. Didn't look close at it. Picture of a child, I think.

The supervisor soon takes control. He doesn't take any shit from anyone. He's doing all the talking. I guess he's telling them that it's no one's fault, that Eleanor wasn't fit enough for the job, and that if they want to keep their jobs they'd better get to work. After a few minutes the local workers pick up their secateurs, wander into the rows. Maria is picking grapes two rows from me, and I hear her crying and muttering for the next hour.

At morning break, I sit on the ground next to Jerome because I have a question I want to ask, if I can pluck up the courage. He turns and gives me a hard stare. I stop chewing my bread. Have I annoyed him? He usually sits on his own. The bread goes pasty in my mouth as I wait for him to speak. Is he telling me to piss off? There's a deep frown line down his forehead. He says, "That fucker of a supervisor." He shakes his head. "My last day here, I'm going to flatten him. You just watch."

I start chewing again. "How did she die?" I ask after I've swallowed.

"Simple: dehydration, heatstroke. That's all."

"Simple?"

He ignores me. He takes a wedge of cheese and bites off half of it.

I don't push for more. After a couple more mouthfuls, he says, "Maria said it was organ failure. That's the end result of dehydration and heatstroke. Her temperature was out of control. She wasn't treated soon enough. I guess she suffered kidney failure, possibly a stroke, multiple organ failure and sepsis."

"I saw Maria trying to cool her down."

"Not enough. She needed a cold bath, stripped down, with ice in the water."

"Are you, like, a nurse?"

He stares at me again. "Eat your food, kid."

We sit in silence. The runner is recharging everyone's water bottle at top speed, like he's suddenly remembered that's his job. The break will end soon, and I take my chance. "Jerome?"

He half turns his head but doesn't speak.

Hesitating, I say, "I liked her. Eleanor. She said it was a shame I was eighteen. Why did she say that?"

He snorts. "She was fishing. Everyone knows you're younger than that. The boss needed extra hands when you showed up. It suited him to believe you." He takes his enamel cup, pours a refill of wine and sits back down. "Eleanor's a nosey bitch. Sorry, *was* a nosey bitch," he says. "She faked being friendly. I can always tell. Wouldn't surprise me if she informed for immigration. Nice little sideline for a local picker. If she hadn't collapsed and died, I was going to confront her. Question is, kid, if you're under eighteen, a minor, why don't you hand yourself in?"

I'm about to speak but I suck in my lips. I keep doing this. Wanting to trust people. Skylark, Ma Lexie, Odette. Then Eleanor, if I can believe

Jerome. Was she an informer? It's lonely when you can't trust anyone. I look Jerome in the eye. "I want to find my parents. My father left Spain and headed to Manchester, but my mother didn't hear from him after a few weeks. We set off to find him, but my mother and I got separated on the road."

Jerome sighs, like he's heard enough hard-luck stories. "Listen. If you want to find your parents, the quickest way is to hand yourself in. At the reception centres, they check everyone's DNA against their databank. If either your mother or father, or both, are already in the system they'll reunite you."

"And if they're not? What's it like at the reception centres?"

He shrugs. "Never been in one, have I?" He shifts around. "If there's no DNA match they'll ship you out unless you're a minor. Got any papers?"

I've told him enough. "My parents had the papers."

"Look, it's dangerous, you wandering around the countryside. There's scum out there looking for kids on the loose."

The runner blows a whistle. Jerome gets to his feet. I dip my head, pull the neck of my T-shirt and sniff. Am I scum? During my first week, the supervisor told me I "stank to high heaven." Told me I'd infect the entire harvest if I didn't clean up. He said if I didn't take regular showers he'd ban me from the farmhouse dinner on Saturday evenings. Didn't know what he was talking about, but I didn't ask, didn't argue even though I *did* take a shower on my first day, but I was the last in the queue so the water was cold. I flicked the water at my skin, didn't wet my hair, and I had no soap. Every morning, I now check the camp washbasins before setting off to the field, to see if anyone has left a bar of soap behind. I haven't had to buy any yet. And I try to beat everyone to the first shower when our picking finishes. I'm much cleaner and it's worth it. The farmhouse dinner on my first Saturday was the best food I'd eaten since I left home.

———

It's my fourth farmhouse dinner, and I've been thinking about it all day like everyone else. Before I reach the courtyard, I smell chicken roasting on the spit in the open air. I'm one of the last workers to arrive because I'm nervous about where to sit. Four long trestle tables are set out in the open air, each with pitchers of wine and water, baskets of bread, and candles for later. A white rose tree spreads over the entrance door to the house. What I like best is the tree by the winery—it's not the tree itself, it's the three lights hanging down from the branches. For our Saturday dinner the owner puts paper lampshades over the bulbs, and the courtyard feels like a different place. Like a secret grotto.

I edge into the courtyard through an arched entrance, wide enough for a transporter, and I try to imagine the olden days with horses and carts bringing grapes from the fields. Usually I sit with the older women because I know they won't mind me tagging along. The one time I sat with the younger men and women they wanted me to drink more and more wine, and I threw up on the walk back to the camp. I stand just inside the courtyard, close to the winery wall, and look across the tables. Jerome is sitting with the winery workers and he spots me. He points to the bench opposite him. I'm pleased and it must show because he smiles. As I sit down, he says to the others, "This is the lad. He might do it." He turns to me. "They need help in the winery. It's less money than fieldwork, so no one's interested. Easier work though. Sweeping up and hosing down. General dogsbody."

"Dogsbody?" I ask.

"General helper. Have a think about it."

I look around at the winery workers, who have cleaner clothes than the pickers, and I wonder if they're a good team, if they'll be nice to work for. None of them stay in the camp. They must live locally, or they're members of the family and live in the farmhouse.

"Decide tonight, hey?" says Jerome.

I answer with a small nod. I'm not sure. Will they boss me around all day? At least in the fields I'm snipping away at the vines on my own.

"Any volunteers to serve? I did it last week," says a woman with dark, straight hair and dark eyes who I'd mistake for being Spanish, only she has a perfect, neat English accent.

"Me and the kid will do it," says Jerome. It makes sense as we're sat at the end of the bench. We both swing around and make our way to the trestle table outside the farmhouse kitchen. Three salads per table. With those delivered, we head off to the spit, where one guy is pushing the cooked chickens off long skewers while a second guy chops them into quarters with a cleaver. Jerome says, "Twelve for us." The chopper guy pushes our quarters onto two steel platters.

Back at our table, I set the platter down in front of the woman with the straight, dark hair. She's talking, everyone is listening, so I guess she's in charge somehow. She taps the point of her knife on the table. "My grandmother says it's a choice of problems. She prefers the problems we can handle here ourselves." She goes on, but I'm lost because she uses words I don't know and talks in long, long sentences. I can tell she's losing the other workers, too, because they stay quiet and concentrate on the food. She's talking nonstop about the grape harvest, bottle numbers, and I catch "payback." I've heard that before, but the payback *then* meant a good beating.

The chicken is perfect, so juicy. Jerome reaches for the breadbasket and drops two chunks onto my plate. "Eat up," he says in a low voice, as if he's angry. The chatty woman is still talking. She stabs the table again, and that's when I click that she must be chipped, implanted. She's super smart but hasn't noticed that everyone's stopped listening. Can't imagine me getting that mouthy with big words.

Then Jerome surprises me by picking up the conversation. "So, you agree with your grandmother? Stay low-tech." He's been listening all along. "Hire seasonal workers because the risk of a labour shortage is solvable compared to the problems that come with automation, where you depend on remote third parties, often in other countries."

"Yeah. Some teenager in North Korea scheduling the overnight machine pickers. It doesn't feel like farming to my grandmother. She's savvy. We upsell our wine because most vineyards in this valley have taken the tech route. We're the sole cultivator of Rondo grapes in this region to handpick, and most of our production is preordered for weddings."

"You're, umm—" He stops himself. His eyes dart, and he stands, grabs the nearest wine pitcher. "Sorry. Pass the other one to Leo."

Jerome stands and gestures *follow me* with his head. "We can't have the workers getting thirsty," he says, and strides away. I take a huge bite of chicken and follow him. As we reach the winery entrance he says, "This way. Be sharp."

Voices bellow from the far side of the courtyard. I twist around and see a bunch of men and women, all wearing black clothes. Uniforms. One woman is holding up a piece of paper. A whole load of shouting and cussing in the courtyard. Cracking sounds—dishes, glasses, breaking on the cobbles. Jerome grabs me by the arm and rushes me towards the rear of the winery, down a corridor.

He eases open a door. "Immigration raid," he whispers, as he pulls me outside.

"How did you know?"

He puts a finger to his lips. "I saw them. Now move it, or we'll be in prison cells tonight." He bolts across the kitchen garden. Catching up, I grab his arm. "Jerome. Jerome, wait! I can't leave without my stuff."

We keep off the paths in case any immigration officers are positioned in the vineyards. We reach the camping ground and thankfully there's no one else around. We slip into the barn, open our lockers. I grab my backpack, heavy with all the food I'd stashed, and push a bottle of water into the side pocket. I've emptied and refilled the bottle every day since arriving here. Always ready. More important, my backpack still has my papers sewn into the straps.

———

I can still taste the chicken if I suck my teeth. But there'll be no more Saturday feasts in the courtyard. Here I am again walking the canal paths in the moonlight, and this time I'm the teacher. I've told Jerome we walk at night, hide in woodland during the day.

We haven't spoken much, and I realise I don't know anything about Jerome. His English is perfect to my ears, so I don't think he's an illegal. I've decided he's a criminal. Yes, he's in trouble with the police and he's been hiding out in the vineyards.

The wind picks up suddenly and it feels colder. Jerome, ahead of me, stops and waits for me to catch up.

"There's a weather front passing over. Let's speed up," he says. "We'll take shelter if it starts to rain." He looks into the sky, holds out his palm. "Rain's definitely on the way."

He sets off, striding out, and I do my best to keep up, but after a couple of minutes I'm way behind. I can't see him. I have a horrible feeling that we'll meet Odette, as if she's wandering around the canals like a ghost. I know I'm being ridiculous. She'll be long gone. But I'm spooked. Maybe she wasn't as lucky as me, and she's been arrested for murdering her boss. Unless her boss is in a hospital in a coma. Or she woke from a coma and spoke one word: *Odette.*

Can't see Jerome. A few spots of rain are hitting my face. I stop to listen for his footsteps. Can't hear anything over the wind that's whistling in the hedges. I pick up my pace, lengthen my stride. I count my steps on a long bend to pass the time, and when the path eventually straightens, I make out a small bridge over the canal. It's the usual kind of brick bridge on these canals, with a low arch, carrying a quiet country road. The canal path narrows and bends around the brick supports. A white plaque, bright in the moonlight, sits over the bridge arch, with the number 108 printed in black. It's dark under the bridge, and I'm a few steps away when I see Jerome sat there, elbows resting on his knees. I drop my backpack next to him.

"Thought I'd lost you. Where are we?" I ask.

"We've headed north, and now northwest, on the Shropshire Union. We'll rest here a while."

I sit on the damp path. "And then?"

"Lay low for three or four days and then head back to the vineyards, a different one. That's what I'm doing." He turns to me. "*You*, you need to think carefully. This life is temporary for me. To tell you the truth, I'm on the missing-persons list."

I look back at him, my eyebrows shooting upwards, but I can't see his face clearly. "Are you in trouble with—?"

"I need to drop below the radar for a few months," he says. "But you, you can't roam around like me. Anyway, how did you reach the vineyard in the first place? Where've you been living?"

I don't answer him. He doesn't seem bothered that I'm ignoring him. He opens his backpack and pulls out a bag of dried fruit and nuts. Pours some into my palm. He tells me he misses his dog, and I tell him I miss my friends. I'm watching the raindrops on the canal water, and I wonder if a canal can overflow. Jerome says, "Have you any idea how vulnerable you are? You're just a kid." He leans into me and speaks into my ear as if he's telling me a secret. "It's better if you hand yourself in, rather than being caught."

"If I had papers would it make a difference?"

"Sure it would." He nudges me with his knee. "If you've got papers . . ." I ignore him again. "So, assuming you've got papers proving you're a minor"—he lets that hang—"then they can't throw you out of the country. You can take indentured work on the fish farms or the power-from-waste plants outside the enclaves. If you decline that offer, you'll be kept in youth detention and deported as soon as you turn eighteen."

"And if they do find my parents?"

"There's the thing, kid. You've a better chance of staying here, long term, if your parents don't show up. Because if they're not asylum seekers, if they're not actual refugees, they don't stand a chance."

I tell him my parents wanted a new life, and wanted me to get chipped when I turn eighteen, become an office worker and make loads of money. Jerome doesn't interrupt but gives a heavy sigh, and I can tell what he's thinking. He thinks my parents were stupid to have this dream. I ask him straight, "What are my chances of getting chipped?"

He laughs.

"I'm serious."

"Your one chance is this, so listen: Hand yourself in. It looks better. Show the immigration people your documents, take indentures. You'll work for the state until you're twenty-five, minimum. Then apply for right-to-remain and you might have a chance, a slim one, of getting late implantation. But be careful what you wish for, kid. Believe me."

Jerome speaks in a low, soft voice. "Let's rest up during the day tomorrow. Stay hidden. On Monday, I can take you close to a police station and leave you to walk in. Immigration will want to know where you've been living, how you crossed the Channel, who trafficked you, where you've worked, how you've survived. They'll treat you better if you tell a good, truthful story. You should practise it."

And so, I tell Jerome my story under this bridge, number 108. I tell him about all the people I've met because he's the first person to tell me anything helpful, about how it all works. He knows stuff. And I feel sorry for him after he tells me *his* story—that even though he's chipped and, at one time, had a good job, his wife left him.

In any case, I want to tell Jerome my story. I'm tired of all the secrets. You have to trust someone when you're on your own. But I don't mention Odette.

I lean my head back against the damp brickwork of the bridge. In my heart I know the truth, but I can't say the words aloud. My father is dead. If he was still alive, he'd have found a way to contact us while we were still in Spain. Mother didn't have the guts to admit that—to me or herself. When I last saw my mother, she'd already lost her mind. She let me down. Now, I have to do what's best for me.

CHAPTER 6

JEROME

My instincts when I first encountered the boy proved correct. He's a minor. And before he arrived at the vineyard, he'd been serially trafficked. By dragging him away from the farmhouse raid, he instantly trusted me. Indeed, he yielded the name of each person who supposedly helped him on his journey. Once he started talking, all was revealed within the space of thirty minutes. Easier than I expected.

Our close proximity helped. We sat shoulder to shoulder under the bridge as we sheltered from the rain. Pure serendipity: the heavy rain, the low bridge, the narrow path. Almost a cave. My first move seemed to do the trick, telling him I missed my dog. I felt the boy's weight as he leaned into me, and I elaborated about walking with my Jack Russell along the beach in north Wales, how he's one of five brothers that me and four of my friends adopted, how we meet up once a year and let the dogs play together. I told him my dog is the best behaved. He isn't yappy. Almost convinced myself I actually owned a dog.

I switched the conversation around, said I'd watched him at the vineyard and admired his diligence. It was a shame we had to move on. He wiped his eyes, telling me he missed his friends back in Spain. I chose this moment to apprise him of key facts regarding the immigration process for minors, and as soon as he'd absorbed this reality check, I gently reeled the boy in, telling him I'd be able to advise him better if he showed me his papers.

With a hint of hesitation for effect, I myself opened up. I told him I'd abandoned my job in the city as a legal secretary, that I knew most of the law around citizenship and deportations. Told him I was sick of the job, that the long hours had wrecked my marriage, that I'd walked out of the office one Monday morning back in June and hadn't gone back—either back to the office or even back home. He believed me.

"You're chipped?" he asked.

I simply nodded. He sat quietly for a while, then dug inside his backpack, pulled out a flat tin, which caught the moonlight reflecting off the water surface in the canal. I expected the tin to hold his documents, so I was surprised when he lifted out a pair of scissors. He snipped the rough stitching along the strap of the backpack and teased out a folded piece of plastic, which he unfurled to reveal several slightly tattered certificates and a data pearl. The pearl, he said, might be dead after all the rough handling. I studied the paperwork under torchlight. After a couple of minutes of scrutiny, I announced, forcefully, "You'll be fine, *Caleb*." For Caleb is his name, not Leo. "You're safe." Melodramatic, maybe.

We began practising his story. I gave him my best advice: "Stay as close as you can to the truth because you're less likely to make a slip."

He repeated his story and I tested him, played the part of a police officer and then an immigration official. The police, I explained, would interview him and push him into the immigration process, but he needed to be careful because the immigration officers would try to trip him up. They'll look for any inconsistencies with his earlier statements. One slip, any slip, and they'll leverage that mistake and fast-track him to youth detention.

For sure, he'd be in deep shit without his papers proving his age. I recorded each piece of his documentation. He asked why I was doing so. I fobbed him off, saying I'd make a few enquiries in a couple of months' time, check how his case was progressing. At least the authorities would know someone was taking an interest, I said. The fact is, I know how immigration loses documents all the time, either accidentally or through maliciousness, if they take a dislike, if it suits their own ends in terms of meeting targets. I didn't want Caleb to come a cropper. He's a resilient kid living on his wits without a mother or father or an older sibling looking out for him. I can't resist feeling a heap of sympathy towards him. I wouldn't be human if I didn't.

The rain fell as stair rods, which worked in my favour. I needed time to drill down to elicit descriptions of the traffickers, to winkle out Caleb's stories about Skylark, Jaspar, Mr. Ben, Ma Lexie. They're all prime examples of the *agents of misery* we're trying to root out and the prime focus of my undercover work. We need to send a message to these lowlifes: the risks are too great, the penalties are harsh. Bizarrely, the kid was determined to leave Ma Lexie out of his tale. His loyalty was inexplicable, and I told him he could be making a grave mistake by erasing a key character.

However, if Caleb won't shop Ma Lexie, I'll put her in the frame myself. She's my target now. In legal terms, this Lexie woman had kidnapped a minor, held him hostage and forced him into slave work. She hit him "only one time," he said. Some corrupt form of a mother substitute. And Caleb talks about her, and Skylark and all the others, as people he's met along the way, as though he were a wandering knave in some medieval tale. The kid doesn't appear to recognise the fact that he's been trafficked.

———

Wishing Caleb all the best, I give him a gentle push, watch him cross the street and slowly climb five sandstone steps to the police station entrance. The station stands higher and slightly back from the high

street. The building itself is early Georgian. Window boxes with geraniums. A perfect drop-off on a sleepy Monday morning. The super-
wealthy live in these market towns, so an unaccompanied child migrant
will be a novelty. It still irritates me beyond measure that his parents
thought they had a plan. What did their plan actually amount to?
Start walking, hope for the best. He's a good kid, speaks fairly passable
English, so that's a head start.

I stay in position to check he doesn't have second thoughts. No
one enters or leaves the police station for fifteen minutes, so I move
on. What I crave now is a week back home to shed not only the weeks
of crud, but also my cover story. I'll start researching and create a new
cover. Invent my backstory—from vineyard worker to . . . what? Small-
time trader? Someone who could approach Ma Lexie without raising
suspicion. Or, I could enter the enclave with no further ado and carry
out surveillance. I'll work it out.

In the meantime, the police will interview Caleb, pass their notes
to immigration's first-contact team. It's a slow process but at some
point investigations will begin. If Caleb sticks to his story, the police
will identify two individuals for investigation: the kid's first trafficker,
Skylark—based on his thin description of a young woman and her
leather jacket with a feathered collar—and Jaspar at the Enclave W3
Materials Recycling Facility.

As for the vineyards along the Welsh border—all part of Caleb's
story—the police will learn subsequently of immigration's ongoing
covert surveillance. As an undercover immigration agent, I check which
farms are employing illegal itinerants, which labour agencies are sup-
plying them, and then I cherry-pick individual lines of enquiry. Caleb
formed an individual line of enquiry. Ma Lexie is the next.

We'll stop these farms from using labour-intensive methods—
which inevitably attract illegals—and force them to recognise that the
risk of prosecution is high. We won't brook any claim of ignorance;
they're as guilty as their agents in the eyes of the law.

Caleb did ask, somewhat sheepishly, if he should include *me* in his story. "Leave me out," I said. It's what he expected me to say.

My name is not Jerome. And though it's true that I once worked in the legal world, I was no mere legal secretary. No, I am Jake Devereux, a corporate lawyer, a one-time top fee earner. I extricated myself from that rarefied shitstorm of a job exactly twenty-six months ago. I've no regrets on that count. This life suits me.

I call a cab. Destination: Rollstone Estate. Pebble Town to most people.

———

Back in the day, still married, both Beth and I working all hours, we paired the stress of high-octane work with the adrenaline rush of splashing out on major purchases, the trappings of success, the prizes. How else did we justify our professional choices, the lack of a social life, being too tired for sex? She said Sunday mornings ought to be sacrosanct, but we often slept until midday, and we religiously pounded the treadmills on Sunday afternoons. Though, what's the point in looking taut, going to all that effort, spending acres of time and money on bespoke training regimes, if there's no payback in terms of shags per week?

Another major time sink: our never-ending search for a character house that required no renovation work whatsoever, one that suited two corporate lawyers with no time to choose so much as a paint colour. We gave up this endeavour and employed a house scout. That's how we came to live in an architectural gem, our pebble house, on the much-lauded Rollstone Estate.

The scout knew how to push our buttons, for sure, by selling a concept and an aesthetic completely at odds with our tight, cubic work environment. A 3D-printed pebble house embodies curves—a fairy-tale home we simply couldn't resist—emulating the look of straw-bale construction both inside and out.

Whenever I sprawl out on the sofa, I like to imagine a forester wielding a chainsaw, shaping bales with skilled sweeps, creating the living room's rounded window reveals. I see, in my mind's eye, this imaginary forester slapping lime mortar against the straw, smoothing out the final surface to form an organic-textured home. Beth and I loved our printed home—our haven—although we didn't on *any* weekday see our haven during daylight hours. And, as it transpired, this mutual love wasn't enough to keep us together.

I walk from the taxi park through the lush grounds of Rollstone Estate. The scattering of houses appears refreshingly haphazard. I detect an echo of a childhood adventure—piles of stones marking the route through an imaginary jungle. And I feel energised by the contrast between the smooth pebble houses and the compact stands of trees. Have any other residents noticed that all the trees planted by the estate office have compound leaves? Some attached pinnately, others palmately. It's a conscious decision, I'm sure.

Last year, by chance, I came across images of an ancient Portuguese village, Monsanto, famous for the giant granitic boulders that perch over its houses and pigsties. Struck me as oddly similar to our estate. I arranged a surprise holiday. Beth loved the place, until we were forced to return home early. Her job took the blame, but I shouldn't have blustered. It could easily have been my job that pulled us away.

We split the furniture between us. Beth lives on the far side of the estate. Neither of us could bear to leave the area, so we snapped up the first available house, paid well over the odds to secure it, and Beth gave me first choice, stay or move. After all, the split was essentially her decision. I stayed, and I still need to replace some of the furniture she took.

I'm left here in an almost empty living space, rocking in my 1942 Hans Wegner, a museum piece. It occurs to me, in my haven, that I have three unoccupied bedrooms. The third bedroom is the only room on the top floor. I never go up there. I think of young Caleb, a nice kid.

What would be so bad? Caleb or someone like him, living on the top floor, going to school, someone to come home to.

Am I getting soft in my old age?

I message Beth. *Back home. Dinner?*

Half an hour later she replies. *Sorry, Jake, got plans.*

Of course she does. I've heard as much.

We try to keep things civil, Beth and I. She didn't approve of my new job. She said she wouldn't have a child with a guy who lives in two worlds.

———

I laugh at myself as I step into the shower for the third time in twelve hours. Five weeks of vineyard camping reset my standards in personal hygiene. The things I do to fit in. Grime in every crease and crevice. My hair is long and knotted and my scalp's itchy as hell. I can laugh about it because I enjoy my work. How many jobs would allow me to reinvent myself every few weeks?

When I cast my mind back, I thought I'd hit the jackpot winning a senior associate position at Fen 'n' Fletch, that is, Fender and Fletcher. Not simply because of the higher salary, but because I imagined I'd gain control over my workload. I was swiftly disabused of such optimism. The hours were as long, the pressures greater, with deadlines—some real, others fake—every half hour of the day. A tsunami of documents upon documents upon documents. Proofreading, marking, signing. Swamped by requests, I diverted tasks to junior associates who, in turn, diverted grunt work to interns. My first priority was simple: deal with any request from those senior partners who sat on the remuneration committee, deciding bonuses. All other tasks were juggled, delegated, ignored. Before I even reached the office, clients had filled my morning diary with conversation slots, which I couldn't reject. They didn't give a shit about any diary conflicts. Simple solution: I hauled junior associates into these conversations and gave them the job of actually listening, allowing me to read documents for my next meeting, answer new incoming messages while the client blathered. Later, the junior associates gave me a precis of the actual conversation.

Trench warfare, basically.

I rarely dealt face-to-face with my fellow partners or my clients. That was the worst aspect of the job. I had no idea when I chose my area of speciality that corporate law would be so lonesome. Sounded sexy, tailored for high-flyers. I observed my contemporaries working in other departments and comprehended after a couple of years—when the initial buzz connected with corporate law distorted into maddening tinnitus—that I'd taken the wrong path.

It's blindingly obvious, now. The best fit for me was employment law. It's all about people. Meetings, up close and personal, with complainants or defendants, taking witness statements, attending hearings at tribunals. I'd be in my element. The drama of it all. Last-minute discussions with witnesses outside the tribunal, attempts to secure an eleventh-hour settlement. Real people, real-world problems, real human stories.

Had I taken that path, I'd have kept the best cases. Whereas, in corporate, two departmental simulants—our genetic superiors, supposedly—took the highest value work and were constantly breathing down our necks. The nadir of my corporate law career: I'm pulled up in front of the senior director for productivity, and he lists the oversights, inaccuracies and missed deadlines in my previous three months' work as logged by the HR simulant, Nadia. None of my oversights or omissions was significant. But I suppose if Nadia can measure something, she's going to fucking measure it.

Measure my dick!

No, in employment cases, empathy skills are critical. As good as the latest simulants are—far fewer recalls than three or four years ago— they can't cajole a nervous witness to take the stand, or persuade an aggrieved client to accept a deal. If I were in charge at Fen 'n' Fletch,

I'd keep all the simulants in the back room in support roles like Nadia's; if Nadia developed a glitch we could simply ship her out, cancel the lease. No need to explain to clients about the sudden disappearance of a simulant.

———

Midday on Thursday I cook myself a three-course lunch at home. This is the upside of undercover work; although I spend weeks on operations, I rack up time in lieu, and after the vineyard reconnaissance I'm content to spend time at home rather than chase off on holiday. What could be better than rediscovering my old self in beautiful, calm surroundings? I'm living the dream. I wish my old colleagues at Fen 'n' Fletch could see me.

I'm clearing the dishes when I receive a report from external operations on the immigration sweep of Bowens' vineyard. The appendices are my main interest: a list of undocumented workers detained following the raid, and an additional list of those workers with incomplete documentation. I recognise them all from the mug shots. But, who'd have guessed? Here's Maria, who led the remonstrations following Eleanor's collapse and consequent death. So Maria, supposedly local, has been flagged up for incomplete, that is, suspect documentation. I had assumed she'd lived in the area for decades, but I expect she won't be around for much longer. Tough luck.

I dictate a reply:

"Point of information. I vacated the courtyard at the onset of the raid and took with me a young male illegal worker, Caleb Cordova, an unaccompanied minor in fact, who had worked at the vineyard under an alias. I judged that I could elicit specific intelligence from the boy—which the immigration service might fail to do—since I had nurtured a relationship. As soon as I had gathered this intelligence, I escorted him to the police station in Tarporley, having persuaded the boy to surrender himself and cooperate with the authorities. He is now in the system, and I have a new line of investigation in Enclave W3: the subject is an adult female, known to the boy as Ma Lexie, who illegally employed him in the textile trade, as slave labour, and whose involvement the boy is reluctant to reveal to the police or immigration."

———

The strawberry stain on the cutting board is the same shape as Australia. You need a fertile imagination in my line of work, and I have that in spades, according to my aptitude tests at immigration. I came across the job by accident when I opened a news story about migration from southern Europe. I expected to read an article about migratory birds, but it turned out to be an exposé on migratory *people* leaving the Mediterranean rim. At the time, I thought *hard chips*—you all enjoyed the good times. My eye was caught, at the bottom of the story, by an advertising prompt: *Good with people? Ever thought of working in the immigration services?* That's where my journey began. I contacted the recruitment agency and insisted on proceeding with an application, despite the young recruiter's incredulity: "But, you are vastly overqualified."

It's brought me here. At home in the middle of the afternoon, in the middle of the week—never happened in my previous job. I'm lying on a bare maple floor staring at an antique Moroccan wall hanging, triangular motifs with a wild range of hues and hand-stitched, wave-like lines unifying the whole. I track the waves, relax and dictate my full report on my undercover vineyard operation, followed by a formal complaint to our external operations manager because I'm a stickler for procedure. The raid on the vineyard occurred one whole hour before the agreed time for the operation, I point out. I'd even messaged my manager the night before to confirm the start time. What's the point in me undertaking surveillance, I complain, if they ignore my intelligence?

The courtyard dinner had only just started when the raid began. If the officers had held back, the pickers would be on their second or third glass of wine—the evening in full swing—and they'd be slower to react. I imagine some of the illegals escaped. Not only that, external ops must recognise that I was wrong-footed. I had my own game plan, to extricate Caleb, and I needed to grab him at the start of the raid.

———

The shuttle pulls out of Manchester Southern Terminus towards Enclave W3. I'm heading for the Saturday market and aim to arrive at midday when the market is at its busiest. Until I started this job, I gave no thought to the enclaves. Occasionally glimpsed at a distance from a car, or from the air, they squat beyond the metropolitan centres and suburbs. Out there, literally. They didn't even encroach on casual conversation. I regarded them—if I can conjure my former mindset—as new towns built on green fields in the open countryside. How fortunate for them. News channels rarely covered any goings-on in the enclaves, which only confirmed my assumption that these were dull dormitory towns that, of course, I had no reason to visit. They certainly didn't figure in my mind as no-go areas. The fact is, I didn't mix socially with anyone housed in those places. Overlaps in our worlds occurred when I pulled an all-nighter at Fen 'n' Fletch. Office cleaners would appear after midnight, disappear soon after two o'clock, presumably heading home to one of the enclaves.

A couple of my schoolmates, I can only assume, must live out in the enclaves somewhere. They were rejected for cognitive chipping. We all swore we'd keep in touch, but after a couple of years it became hard work even watching cricket matches together, not that they noticed. Their match analysis was so piss-poor. I decided I should move on. It felt kinder for the long run because I could see their trajectories.

My parents maintain closer contact with manual, fully organic workers. But then, my parents are stuck in the past. They have a gardener and chat with him as if they're old friends. He lives in quarters tucked away by the side of their vegetable garden. Such a blatant servile setup; it makes me cringe just to think about it. I don't understand what they're trying to prove. And I particularly dislike how they moderate their vocabulary. I told them a while ago, "If you want to chat with the guy, don't talk down to him." They're from a different era, more practised in the art of condescension.

I'm well versed in enclave life now, though my parents would be alarmed if they knew. I haven't told them much about my work. I let them believe it's mainly a desk job. Previously they were aghast at the long hours I worked, and I don't wish to give them another issue to fixate on—the dangers that they imagine lurk along every alley and street in the enclaves. If I told them some of the sights I'd witnessed, they'd lap it up because people like my parents take such a prurient interest in the underclass. To be fair, I've never heard either my mother or father talk of an underclass. If you don't name it, you can pretend it doesn't exist.

The shuttle zips out beyond the suburbs, and I look out for the sandstone ridges where I walked as a teenager with a bunch of friends. Must be over twenty years ago. We followed the footpaths through fields and hiked up and along the ridge before dropping down for a pub lunch and a couple of pints. One of my old mates, a lawyer himself now, tried to retrace the walk last year, but it didn't work out; the footpaths didn't connect up as they did before. Farmers had taken the opportunity to have the paths declassified. But you can still walk on the ridges and along the canals, so it's no big deal.

It's my first visit to W3, but I've found these enclaves are all much of a muchness. Like these shuttle carriages, they're cheap and cheerful, but I wouldn't want to travel beyond W3 on these slatted seats.

———

I buy coffee from a street vendor and loiter on the cracked and uneven pavement to watch the world go by, giving me time to acclimatise to the market. The street is packed with shoppers, and the smell of dust and body odour is pungent. No one seems remotely interested in me. I'm nondescript, sporting the enclave "look" of faded shirt and shorts, part of my collection of shabby clothes—enclave-chic—kept at home in vacuum-storage bags. My hair's too glossy after a week at home, so I'm wearing an old football cap. I won't shower while I'm here.

The coffee vendor, I decide, runs a neat business. His capital equipment comprises a trolley with a heated urn of water and a set of metal cups attached by chains to his trolley. He's basically selling hot water, and he's serving nonstop. Now that's what I call a stress-free job, one that leaves the entrepreneur with a sense of satisfaction at the end of the working day. Unless it's a front for illegal earnings in some other operation. Unless he's gone into debt to buy the gear. Unless he's paying protection to a local racket. Who knows? The police don't dig into enclave matters if they can possibly avoid it. That's why we in immigration must force the pace on occasion.

After I'm finished, I hand the empty cup to the vendor, and he dunks it in a bucket of soapy water. I merge with the slow-moving crowd and run through my plan: find the clothing section of the market, look for a specialised stall of recycled fashion, check who's working on the stall—I will not approach her at this stage—and follow the target at the end of market day. Once I know where she lives, I'll send a small sparrow drone up to her rooftop, see who's working up there. Should be a cinch to build a case against her, prove that she's connected to Jaspar's recycling operation.

Up ahead I see a pink sheet hanging limp above the heads of the shoppers. I've seen similar primitive signalling in other enclaves, marking the textiles section of the markets. In W5, it's a green sheet. In W9, it's a set of old faded towels pegged on a line across the street. And in

W2, heralding household goods, there's a line strung up with wooden spoons, which clack together on windy days.

I turn into the street below the pink sheet, which is decidedly grubby up close, and ease my way along, neither dawdling nor forcing myself ahead of other shoppers. Mostly junk clothing here. How can people abide buying and wearing any of it? I'm on the lookout for a small-time operation, like this one: a few long scarves, loosely knotted to a bar. It can't be Ma Lexie's stall, based on Caleb's description. It would be far more eclectic.

Ah, brilliant! Three stalls farther down. Fucking sure of it. I dodge between two stalls on the opposite side of the street and thumb through a tangle of second-hand kids' clothes while glancing up to catch sight of the female stallholder. Looks the right age, but I can't get a clear view. She's partly concealed by a male customer. The garments on sale do match the information Caleb gave me: one-offs, hung to display each one individually, rather than jammed together on rails.

Her customer walks off without making a purchase and Lexie, assuming it's her, stares at his back as he saunters away. She plants her hands on her hips. But if she's deflated, her mood switches in an instant. Two women march directly to her stall from my end of the street, and at once Lexie is all smiles. Some banter and then her shoulders shake as she laughs, entirely unrestrained. She's pretty. Fuck, she's stunning.

———

In the hostel dorm, I take a top bunk and stretch out. It's too soon to send up the sparrow. Early evening will be better, when most people are distracted by domestic chores and making meals.

I'm thinking about my subject, Ma Lexie, and not in a fully professional manner. I have a yen for strong women. More specifically, physical strength in a lightweight, small-framed woman. I watched Lexie dismantle her stall midafternoon, manhandling large boards and steel poles, stacking them neatly at the side of the street. She looked lean, her muscles well-defined as though she works out.

I followed her as she pushed a hand trolley stacked with containers, her stock of garments. The market was frenetic with last-minute shoppers, traders starting to pack up. She came to a sudden halt, set down the trolley, pivoted and walked three or four paces in my direction. I could have kicked myself. She didn't focus on me. She stooped, picked two mangoes out of a box on the ground.

The stallholder called to her, "On the house, those, Lexie."

I'd already swivelled, my back to her, while I inspected a pile of misshapen tomatoes. I'd forgotten my training, followed too closely behind her because I hadn't anticipated any danger. Still, I'd nearly messed up.

She returned to the trolley, and I snuck a glance as she dropped the mangoes into a cloth tote bag, the strap of which dug deep into the flesh between her neck and shoulder. I replay that in my mind—the strap, the flesh.

The subject turned off Clothing Street, and I kept my distance. I observed her come to a halt, as expected, at the recycling yard. She disappeared inside. I stood fifty metres away and grew impatient waiting for her to emerge. Became bored acting like a loafer, leaning against a wall, occasionally biting a fingernail, something I'd never do in real life. She reappeared with the loaded trolley and a large bundle balanced on the top. I nipped into the entrance of a housing block, stood back in the shadow of the staircase and waited for her to walk past. That's when I gleaned that the bundle comprised a sheet wrapped around old textiles, a shirtsleeve poking out, and it looked heavy. Her biceps bulged. What a Trojan.

I tailed her once again. She stopped briefly to converse with someone through an open window, waved goodbye and moved on. About one hundred metres farther along the street, she entered a block of flats and did not reemerge. Two minutes or so later, a pair of window shutters opened on the top floor.

Can't be sure, but I'd hazard a guess that's Lexie's place. And now, I'm holed up in the hostel located in the neighbouring block.

———

At six o'clock I make my move to the hostel's shower block, specifically to the end cubicle with the window. I've executed drone surveillance dozens of times before; all I need is privacy. Here goes. I launch my sparrow from the windowsill and fly it vertically, monitoring and controlling its flight with a small tablet. I spin it, giving me a good indication of activity across several rooftops. I see the usual mix of solar arrays and various small enterprises, some easier than others to identify, like the laundry. I swoop down and notice beehives. Swinging around, I see a roof garden opposite Lexie's block. A good place to set down for a while. That's when I notice that the roof garden is suffering neglect. Tall weeds. Pots with shrunken compost and dry, brittle remains of plants. Someone's bored with gardening? Never have understood why people put so much time into gardens; it all goes to rack and ruin eventually, when the owner falls ill, dies. Still, it's odd that this garden is neglected. Must be a story there.

Looking across at Lexie's roof, I linger and monitor for any sign of movement. There's none. Leo—or *Caleb*, I should say—told me about two boys. Where are they? Resting? Time to look closer. I fly the sparrow across the narrow street, circle the roof then drop down to make transects, finally hovering at the entrance to a makeshift structure. This is the workshop that Caleb described. Inside there's nothing but a table with textiles, one chair, no sign of children or bedding. Nothing at all to corroborate his story.

I find that I'm not disappointed.

I'll take a closer look at the window. See if Ma Lexie does live there. The sparrow sweeps over the side of the roof parapet and around the building to the window. Hovering. It's *her* all right. She's singing and swaying as she clears her kitchen table. I increase the volume and zoom in. A mango stone and a discarded mango skin, crosshatched with cuts. She sashays closer to the window, drops the mango waste into a compost dish and looks out of the window. I'm looking into her eyes and she forgets the words to the song. *La la la laa.*

Little wonder that Caleb felt conflicted. Should I leave her be?

———

Sunday morning, and I'm checking out of the hostel when I ask the warden, "Have you noticed the building up the street? The one with the rooftop garden? It's gone to ruin. I can see that from the street. I'm thinking they need a gardener."

He shrugs. He pays little heed now that I've checked out.

"See, I'm a gardener. Who's the janitor in that building? I'll offer my services."

He turns away and talks to the wall. "Don't know the whole sodding street, mate."

I walk up the street towards the market square where I'll stroll by Lexie's stall again. A message comes in from Beth:

I called by. No sign of life. What about that dinner?

What's this, then? I message straight back because I don't do mind games with Beth. She'd see straight through me.

Finishing up some fieldwork. Back later today. I'll book somewhere special.

And a reply: *Good. I'd like to chat.*

And a follow-up: *I think I miss you.*

I whistle long and low. No point sticking around here. I don't *need* to do these specials, these forays. I'm not chasing promotions any longer.

But I can't resist making contact with Lexie, if only briefly.

I saunter up to her stall while she's finishing up with a customer. Lexie's speaking voice, accent and all, is not as soft as her singing voice.

Her teeth could do with some work. I'm tempted to buy a remake blouse for Beth, but I stop myself. I don't like to mix business with pleasure. The customer walks off, and I'm left facing Lexie. A breeze wafts her dress, and I detect body odour. Brings me to my senses. I say, "It's nice, this blouse, but I'm not sure. Definitely in the running." I half turn to walk away but hesitate. "Say, do you make all these clothes yourself? It's great workmanship."

I wonder if she's ignoring me. She refolds the garments on the tabletop. She turns her back to me and says, "Yes. All my own work. Thanks!"

God, she seems harmless enough. Anyway, I'm wasting my time without any evidence from her rooftop.

I head off to the shuttle station, updating my report on this Ma Lexie woman en route:

No evidence of illegal employment.
Line of enquiry closed.

CHAPTER 7

JASPAR

Old Frankie crosses the yard, approaching my office with a jaunty spring in his step. I chortle to myself. He never gives up, does Frankie. Still serving the clans at his age.

He's chuffed with himself, quite rightly. I won't deny him his moment of glory, even if he only did yesterday what he's bloomin' paid to do—paid not just by me but by all the clans. He's supposed to clock any interlopers. Worth every penny we cough up to pay for his coffee stall. On the edge of the market, it's a handy spot to see who's coming from and going to the shuttle station.

He steps into my office. Hiding any feeling of satisfaction, he says, deadpan, "Hey, Jasp. What's going on, then?"

"Under control, Frankie. Thanks for enquiring. Here's a bonus for the prompt action yesterday." I pass him a stack of enclave credits. Knew he'd call by at some point, so I had the stack ready.

"I seen your boys this morning, leading that fella off," he says.

"I doubt he'll be back." I give Frankie a wink.

A skinny devil these days, but in his prime, before his injuries *reduced him,* shall we say, everyone gave Frankie his due as a serious fixer. Even now, though he's way down the ladder, he takes pride in his work. I like that about him. If my dad had took one-fifth the pride in his work that little Frankie took today, we'd have a fucken empire. Any road up, I'm a patient man whatever anyone thinks, and I know I'll get there in the end. It's all about patience, hard work and managing risk. Managing, in other words, other people's balls-ups. It's Lexie's balls-up that's back at the top of the agenda.

"That fella—what a wanker, eh Jasp? Trying to pass for a local. He weren't fooling no one, were he? Thought he could stroll in here on his own, the wanker. Did Lexie tell you, wore a dirty Man City cap? Talk about disrespectful. That's what I thought."

This could go on, so I stand, place my hand on his shoulder and edge him to the door. "Job well done, mate. We'll take it from here." I'm thinking, mind, without little Frankie I'd be right exposed. I'd have no inkling that someone was snooping around.

As it turned out, once we got the nod from Frankie, everything went like clockwork. Classic example of old-fashioned surveillance by foot soldiers who know their patch. Frankie sends his chaser, a woman called Trace, to follow the interloper. She messages back to Frankie that the guy's lurking in Clothing Street, eyeballing Lexie. Trace knows her job well enough. She signals a girlfriend, and the two of them go over to Lexie, all best-mates-like, tell her to make a show of laughing with them, tell her to watch out for the bugger in the Man City cap.

Last night, nine o'clock or so, I pieced everything together, all the local intel about . . . what shall I call him? Lexie's stalker? Stalker Man. Yeah. This intel includes Lexie's own account of what happened. She comes to the yard straight after the market. Tells me, when Trace and her mate gave her the warning, she straightaway spotted Stalker Man hanging around by the second-hand clothes stall a bit further up Clothing Street. He wandered off at one point, she tells me, but then reappeared midafternoon while she was busy dismantling the stall and stacking her trolley. So she sets off to deposit her takings in my safe, and the silly cow decides to catch him in the act of following her. Came fucken face-to-face, but she claims she didn't catch his eye. I told her straight, she was idiotic. I had Trace and two of my lads following him. I didn't need *her* playing the sleuth. Naturally, I had to satisfy myself there were no monkey business, so I asked Lex: Do you know the fucker? Said I'd only ask her once. She claimed she didn't know him, and I believed her.

Anyways, according to my lads, this Stalker Man follows Lex from the market down the street towards my yard and later follows her from the yard to her block of flats. He checks into the hostel in the neighbouring block to Lexie's. Seriously, I didn't like hearing that.

Lexie then drops the bombshell in a message, a couple of hours after she gets home, that she thinks a bird drone is hovering outside her kitchen window. "Peeping Tom?" I ask. "No," she says. "I'm clearing up the kitchen. I'm not swinging from the goddamn chandelier. Why would it be hovering watching me wash the dishes?"

No sleep for me last night. I stayed at the yard, double-checking through all the employee records, making sure all the warehouse workers are bona fide local. See, I shipped out the underage workers, including those two little nippers of Lexie's. Transported them to labour agents within twenty-four hours of Caleb's disappearance. See, if Caleb was picked up, he'd shop us without a doubt. And the penalties are grievous for keeping underagers on your premises. But they'd still need evidence.

Two days after shipping out the underagers, I took the plunge. Right off the top board. I shipped out *all* the illegals. Not sure it was totally necessary because, soon after, my man in the police tells me they picked up the Odette girl on the roadside, across the border in Wales. He says she claimed physical abuse and enslavement, but no one in the force gives a shit. She's had a summary judgment, he tells me, and she's off to a detention facility, ready for shipping back home. Wherever that is. No one's wasting money on any trial for the murder of an enclave resident, he says. In any case, the janitor woman was breaking the law in the first place. And the police don't care unless an enhanced some-one or other is mugged or murdered. More to the point, as far as I was concerned, my man tells me there's no mention in the case notes of any accomplice.

Question is: Has this Odette been kicked out yet? Immigration might still be screwing her for info, making false promises because that's their fucken job to do so. And who is Stalker Man? Is this fella a real-life creep, taken a shine to our Lex? I hope so because that's the easiest problem to fix. My inclination, however, is that Odette has talked some more, or Caleb has been picked up and he's doing the talking. It's my job to sweat over these things even though, thanks to me, our exposure is near zero. Even if immigration raids these premises in the next five minutes, they'll find nothing suspect. But, hell's fucken teeth, profits are well shite, and they'll stay like that until I can restaff the conveyors with Skylark's help.

———

Inside the recycling plant, I climb the steel steps to the foreman's office, the air getting more and more fetid the closer I get to the top of the building. I come up here at least twice a day. I like to look down on the conveyor belts. All second-hand machinery. We now have our own workshop in the yard to print spare parts because the conveyors need coaxing, always something breaking down. But it's way better than in my dad's day. My dad didn't spend on machines. Back then, I'd come in here and it was total Armageddon, as if all the beggars north of the fucken equator were either in the warehouse or outside in the yard picking through piles of recycling. Became a laughing stock among the clans. If me and Ruben hadn't stepped in, the family would have lost the collection and sorting contract, which was unheard of—a clan family losing their contract. No way were me and Ruben going to let that sorry state come to pass. Didn't give Dad a choice. We eased him out, telling him he'd developed a bad problem with his left knee. Ruben told him to start practising his limp.

I like watching the blowers on the first separation line. It's simple, like a child worked it all out. A blast of air from below sends the light-weights shooting up, and they're sucked into a huge pipe leading to another conveyor for more separation. So simple. Fucken poetry if you ask me.

Up here, I feel like the boss. And I'm reminded of looking down on Lexie's stall this morning, waiting for Stalker Man to show his face again. I requisitioned a flat on the opposite side of the street for the whole of the Sunday market. Midmorning, the market is teeming when Stalker Man shows up, and this time he walks right up to the stall. He's wearing a different cap, so I don't know it's him. Not until Lexie gives the signal. She takes a blue-and-red-check shirt, folded at the back of the stall, and shakes it out, puts it on a hanger and hangs it from the pole above the front table. She fiddles with the sleeves, straightening them, and I'm hoping she doesn't fiddle so much that the pin mic drops out. All I can hear is the market clatter. After he's messed about for half a minute, he says, "It's nice, but I'm not sure."

I gave Lex a long talking-to beforehand. Told her not to speak to the guy unless she really had to, in case the bastard had a mic himself.

I'm looking down on her from the first-floor flat. She smiles at him and carries on rearranging the clothes that are laid out flat on the table. He's still hanging around. He says, "Do you make all these clothes yourself? It's great workmanship." She turns her back, appearing rude, and I can't hear what she says. When she doesn't turn around, he wanders off.

He's several metres away when Lex looks up at me at the window. I felt weird, cut up. Because here was I. There was Lex, all wide-eyed like she's asking if she's still in trouble with me. But all I can think of is my brother, Ruben. Hits me like a punch in the chest, my duty to him. It's like Ruben's angry with me right there in that moment for not taking proper care of his widow. Reminding me to look after his Lex. So, I give her the thumbs-up. And I'm grinning. Not because I'm happy but because I'm thinking of what Ruben would likely do if he suddenly materialised. I can see him charging down the market, shoulders forward, and ready to flick his knife at Stalker Man. Ruben would be on it. That fucker wouldn't even reach the station. I guess that's why Ruben's dead and I'm not, because I think things through for three seconds longer. Even so, I decided not to take any chances with Stalker Man, the smarmy git.

Ruben was our man on the street, only too happy to sort out trouble. Jeez, we sorted out some shit when we took over. First off, Ruben had to stop the other refuse clans weaselling on our streets, nicking from our bins. Taking the piss, they were. It took about two months for the message to get through loud and clear that Ruben and me had took over, and that Ruben was getting handy. He got the problems more or less sorted. I told Ruben he could give up his night-time patrols, but I should have put my foot down and told him to delegate to one of the cousins. Thing is, I think he liked catching the pilferers. I think he liked a bit of knife work, knowing the police wouldn't make much effort. But when Ruben was murdered, I almost didn't care after that. I hadn't protected my kid brother. If it weren't for our sister, Amber, the blockhead cousins would have taken the reins at the yard, and we'd all be back to where we started. Amber got me straightened out, like she did when Mum died.

The main conveyor judders and stops. Another breakdown. The workers are whooping and hollering, and when the technician runs through the warehouse, she's met with catcalls and whistles. Doesn't deserve it. She's better than the last tech—a migrant who claimed to be some shit-hot engineer. But I saw through him in the end. A fucken bullshitter. Made one excuse too many, so I threw him on the main conveyor, and it still makes me laugh, how he totally panicked. Arms and legs going like an insect on its back. Couldn't right himself and ended up in the big drum separator. So fucken hilarious. Course, I let him out after he'd tumbled for a couple of minutes. Crushed a couple of fingers, which probably had to come off, but we didn't see him again.

No, this new tech, she's doing okay. I *could* roll up my sleeves, but them days are behind me, and in any case, it's time for the family's weekly gathering.

———

My man Greg stands at the corner of the market square. He never comes to the yard. That's my cast-iron rule. He falls in next to me, and we saunter down in the direction of my sister's place. I'm nervous delegating jobs to Greg, jobs I'd have handed to Ruben once upon a time. Ruben was careful, worked alone as often as he could. Preferred to have lookouts instead of going in mob-handed. He had real confidence that way in his own abilities.

"You got the message, then? All sorted," says Greg.

I nod my head, and he gives me the full verbal. He reports that he and his mate grabbed the interloper at the back end of the market and pushed him along the alley leading to the market's rubbish skips. Cut open his pockets before he knew what was happening, made him open his phone. Had some fancy credit apps, so the game was up—he wasn't no local. After a bit of close questioning, about what business he had coming to the enclave, he gives some bullshit answer about being a writer doing research. Greg's mate went through his messages and asked if he was rushing home for dinner with lovely Beth. And was this a photo of her?

Greg laughs and says, "Jasp, you should have seen the fucken colour leave his face. I knew we didn't have to cut him. Right tempting though. Just roughed him up."

"How did you leave it, then?"

"I said if he shows his face or writes anything about our enclave, we'll be looking him up, and Beth of course. I told him we'd insist on a fucken invite to dinner."

———

Amber, my kid sister by six years, is the one family member who dares give me lip. She holds out her hand to each of us in turn, and we slap our credits into her palm. She tells me I still owe for last week and sends her current live-in, Freda, to fetch our food order for our Sunday roundtable. Except there's no round table. Amber has a small square kitchen table and four chairs. On Sundays, she borrows two more from a neighbour. The six chairs are squeezed in so that my dad and his two brothers sit uncomfortably close. They always sit at the table—but only at my say-so. The other three chairs are taken by me, Amber and, since Ruben died, by Lexie. The rest of the tribe either stand or sit on the edge of Amber's bed.

I eye my dad's two younger brothers, who work the grunt side of the business—rubbish collection—and it still narks me that they're benefitting from mine and Ruben's hard work, turning around the whole business. Their kids reap the reward too—cousins Jeff and John who do the day-to-day rotas for collection, repairs on bicycles and trailers. All routine. Cousin Trish, on other hand, brings proper value to the business. She's carved out a space for herself as a fixer. She doesn't get physical, but she keeps close to the people who could mess things up for us: housing staff in the enclave administration, weighbridge officers at the power plant. She makes it her business to know everyone.

When Ruben died, rumblings got back to me via Amber that the three cousins thought one of them should sit in Ruben's chair at our Sunday roundtables. I knew Trish could make a good case for joining the inner circle. She has a way with words, pretty smart, and I suspect at some time in the past she's slipped off to some fucken charm school. As for Jeff and John, I felt like going round, right then and there, and knocking some sense into them, the planks. The family members that count are Dad, me, Amber and Ruben's widow. And as I see it, Lexie is keeping the chair warm for when my eldest turns twenty-one, or twenty-five. I haven't decided when exactly. I'll see how he shapes himself.

Five years ago, these gatherings were total mayhem. There were too many damned people in the room. Even my dad's old cousins came along for the banter and a couple of free beers. Freeloaders. They had fuck all to say. When me and Ruben took over, we told them it was a new business model, which seemed to dazzle them because no one had ever talked in business-speak. We told everyone that modern businesses operate with a small board of directors of key decision-makers. Sure, we buttered up the uncles and cousins. Told them they'd be important to the business just as before, and our door was always open, blah blah. But the subtext was this: they were out, and we were in.

All my dad's cousins and their adult kids, some of them older than me, still work in the operation, but well down the food chain. Some distant relatives, those lurking at the bottom of the gene pool, work on the collections, that is, pedalling fucken bicycle trailers, with a weekly bonus to save face within the family. Up until a year ago, Dad was giving me one sob story after another, that second cousin's great-niece, or whoever, was struggling and could we find her some extra hours, or some such crap. I told Dad to put all them appeals through Amber, and she'd run through the cases with me once a month. I don't want to be mithered all the time. It's unproductive.

I don't allow family members to bring partners to these gatherings. They ain't real family, and these blow-ins know the score from the kick-off. Lexie is included, out of respect for Ruben, and I've put her in charge of spin-off business. She isn't *actually* in charge of spin-offs. But *saying so* allows me to sit her at the table.

Freda comes back with the food, calls each person's name, passes out their order, and makes herself scarce. Amber has her well trained.

The agenda's in my head, as we don't write nothing down, and I kick things off quick.

"Right then. You might have heard that we've had an unwelcome visitor snooping around this weekend, just when I thought everything was settling back to normal." Lexie looks down and I reckon I can hear her stomach churning. "Anyways, we've dealt with it." I look around the room and notice my dad pulls in his chin, and I've known that dubious look since I was a kid.

He chips in, "You want to go easy. Keep a low profile, I say. We've nothing to hide. Not now." All he wants is a quiet life.

"Which brings me to the next item on the agenda," I say. Keep it short, keep it sweet. "I want you all to double-double-check that all the folk on our books are legal. I don't care about freelancers, because that's their problem. But anyone on a regular wage needs rechecking. I'll do my own rechecking at the yard right after this meeting. And we'll stay legal for another three months. Then I'll look at the situation again."

Dad's brother Nicky, who organises payroll for the trailer cyclists, says, "If the profits are down, will family members working on the trailers still get their bonuses?"

"No worries. Things aren't that tight." Sweats over nothing, does Uncle Nicky. "Where we're hurting bad is at the yard. Labour costs have shot up with us recruiting more locals. But I'm running things lean. I've talked this over with Dad." I *did* talk things over with Dad, but only so I could come here and say so. I've no interest in his opinion. "For the next few weeks, we'll operate undermanned. We won't match our usual recycling rates, but I don't want a fucken mountain of recyclables spilling out into the yard." I give Dad the look, to say we're not going back to the old days. "We're adding some recyclables to the waste we send for incineration at the power plant."

Trish raises a hand. "The weighbridge officers will notice. Are you bothered about that?"

"Speak to them. I don't want no spike in our weights. If we're being watched, we want everything as normal."

"I'll tell them to measure actual weight until further notice. We don't want the usual twenty percent bump."

I'm about to move on when she coughs and says, "I'm hearing that the incinerator plant and fish farms are struggling with their own productivity. Seems they've hit a dip in labour supply. So, down the line, won't we face problems ourselves finding migrants?"

Uncle Nicky says, "What? They're running low on migrants? No way."

She says, "Actually, yeah they are, according to my contact. They had a glut of workers when the first fire refugees came over. Until they expanded the fisheries, they didn't know how to keep them all busy. That first wave is close to finishing their indentures. Whereas, the number of migrants coming over has levelled off."

"You could have fooled me," says Dad.

"Say what you want," she says, without sounding rude. "All I know is they're not meeting targets for fish production, and the enclave council will soon put up prices. Wouldn't be surprised if we see demonstrations, with fish being the only sodding protein around here."

I'm wondering if this connects with our snooper, but I keep my thoughts to myself. I like joining the dots without any help. If they're short of migrant workers, immigration will be cracking down on operations like mine, which makes me puke. When the enclave administration makes profits from fish and power generation, those profits get sucked out. When I make profits, the money stays in the enclave. That's how I see it. We're all using migrants. What's the fucken difference?

Lexie pipes up. "Jasp, if that's the way things are going, we should think about better machinery. I don't want migrants working for me again." I'm glad to see her blush. "I could make more money if I had better equipment. I'm thinking, too, about your conveyors. Should we raise money within the family to invest at the yard?"

"Thanks, Lex. See, I like new ideas like that." It don't hurt to throw around a bit of praise, and I'm of a mind to praise Lex. Ruben would like that.

"And like I say . . ." Lex raises her voice. "I don't want illegals working for me, but"—she swallows hard—"I've had an offer. Skylark wants to work with me in the remake business. Hands-on with the sewing. And also as a business partner to help me expand into other enclaves. Would you mind, Jasp?"

A fly lands on the table, walks an inch. I reckon I hear its footsteps, it's so quiet in here. The fly walks another inch.

I'm right fucked off to hear this from Lexie. Before I can speak, she chips in again. "Skylark says she'll find someone else to help you on the labour side, Jasp. She called for a chat during the week. She'd planned to do a final job for her farmers, but she heard about immigration raids all along the border counties. Frankly, she's lost her nerve, ferrying people. I'd have mentioned it sooner, Jaspar, but with all the fuss this weekend . . ."

"Where is she now?" I ask.

"Still on the road, doing normal courier work. Waiting to hear from me about her proposition."

Proposition! I glance above Lexie's head and imagine Ruben stood behind her, his arms folded. He's staring me down. So I look back at Lexie and nod my head. I slap the table—that fly is fucken annoying. "If there's nowt else . . . ? Meeting over."

No one stands to leave because they all have drinks to finish. And I know what's coming. Uncle Nicky will get on to his favourite subject before I can push them all out of the door. Amber squeezes past Dad and fetches a beer bottle. I call across to her, "Not for me, Amber." She knows that means no more beer for anyone. I'm not in a mood for small talk. Bloody Skylark.

Uncle Nicky raps the table with his knuckle, leans forward, spoiling for a scrap. "If the migrants are coming out of indentures in droves, what's going to happen here in the enclaves? Where are they going to live? That's what I want to know."

I tell him to stop fretting about things that don't affect us, that the migrants will get the old enclave flats. *He* wouldn't want to live there. We should see them as a new cheap labour source, and we might need them now that Skylark's gone into *retirement*. But I can't be bothered arguing with Uncle Nicky. He wants something to complain about, is all.

Trish peers round to eyeball Uncle Nicky. "I met my woman in the housing department last week. Took her for lunch. She's partial to lunch meetings. She says the new laws for naturalised migrants will make a difference. She says they've had to act because these migrants often weren't inoculated at birth. And even though they're jabbed as soon as they enter the immigration system, the inoculations aren't fully effective when given to mature adults. Some of these migrants will still have addictive behaviour, and we all know that brings trouble."

She's dead right, there. No one talks these days about the embarrassing grandparents and great-grandparents who were drunks or worse. Trish continues while she has Uncle Nicky on the back foot. "Any naturalised migrant committing a crime, or causing affray, will get five times the tariff that's applied to people born here, and they'll serve their sentences back in a migrant detention centre. Or they can choose deportation instead of incarceration."

I'm thinking about that as I walk back to the yard. See, it don't seem right somehow, not that I'm going feeble in my middle age. These migrants do their indentures and then they're set up to fail. One noisy birthday party and they're dragged in for disturbing the peace. I'd be doing them a favour if I took them under my protection, clan protection. I'll find out where they're being housed, get some recruiters in there. They'll be legal, after all, but they'll need shielding from trumped-up charges. They'll be scared shitless of putting a foot wrong. With clan connections, the police will stay away.

———

I'll catch the sunrise. Call me romantic.

Five hours' sleep is enough for me but, still, sleeping on that lumpy sofa in my office was a bad idea. I should have gone home because I'm aching like I've done a week on the conveyors. I'll walk off the aches and stiffness. Same time, I'll think about the day ahead. Whenever I have a problem nagging at me, this is the time of day I get it straightened out.

I make my way in the dark to the eastern edge of the enclave. It's not far away because the recycling yard is on the eastern outskirts—that means the smells are blown away from the enclave most of the time. It's dead quiet. The first noise of the day will be the bicycle trailers—ours and the other clans'—taking waste to the incinerator plant, but they don't start their back-and-forth until five o'clock.

I'll watch the sunrise then slip back home before the kids wake up, close the door quietly, ease off my shoes and get back in bed. I like it when Yana groans that I'm cold and tries to push me off. But she's so warm, it feels like coming home. Morning sex is the best because I'm too brain fried at the end of the day. Mornings are the only time I feel chilled enough. Sometimes I'm so sick of the pressure, looking out for the whole family. But it's best to be the boss. That's what I keep telling myself, and Yana understands how I feel about the mornings.

I should walk out here more often, and this early. Clears my fucken grey matter. An old heap of a car lies abandoned by the side of the track, and I sit on the bonnet waiting for the sun to lift fully above the horizon. Shouldn't take long. There's enough light to make a silhouette of the giant incinerator, the warehouse at the fish farm and the perimeter walls around the whole camp. I wouldn't ever admit it to anyone, but if I had to choose a labouring job, I'd fancy working on a fish farm. Working beside water appeals to me. Must feel cool even at the height of summer. Better than the dusty heat in our yard. And the fish must be happy enough, until the moment they're sucked out and put on ice. Even then they won't know what's going on.

I've heard it said that you can tell when someone works at the fish farms, not just by the smell but by the state of their nails. You get strong and shining nails as if they're morphing into fish scales. Don't believe that myself. I look down at my own nails. Would people think it strange, like . . . affective, if I kept them clean? I've been thinking about my image, how I need *a thing*. Then people would say, you know Jaspar? The guy with . . . the thing?

If I'd been chipped, I'd know what my thing should be. Tried to come up with something by scanning through images of clan bosses and old-world gangsters, looking for their thing. But it's too hot for most of their trademarks—the clothes, the hats. Clean fingernails though . . .

The sun's sitting on the horizon, and the sky's lightening up. I catch a movement across the ground about thirty metres away. A stray dog probably. I use my heel to dig out a stone in the earth. I pick it up and lob it at the dog shape. I miss the fucker. It moved so fast I reckon it must be a cat, a big un.

I reckon I'll call on Lex this morning and have a chat about a new sewing machine. Whenever I do make a gesture, like if I *do* buy Lex a

machine, I prefer to go over the top. It's my way. You could say that's
my thing. I'll surprise Lex by offering more than she asks for, buy a
brand-new machine instead of a second-hand one. I'll ask her what
else will increase her productivity, or I might even ask if she wants the
bigger flat across the landing. I could sort that out, easy. She did mess
up with them kids, but Amber says I should go easier on Lex because
she's her one close friend. Amber doesn't like to mix too much outside
the family, and she doesn't want Lex to leave the enclave, to go back
home. And seeing Lex, Amber says, helps her to remember Ruben, and
remember how happy Ruben was with Lex.

There's a metallic creaking noise somewhere behind me, and I recognise it straight off. I try to ignore it, but it's getting closer until it's
like a squeaking rat, disturbing my private time, my thinking time.
Comes closer still, until a guy pedalling a rubbish trailer appears directly
alongside me.

I say, "What the fuck you doing out at this time?"

I don't recognise the runt. He's not one of ours. We never send our
trailers out this early.

He looks over his shoulder at me and says something foreign. He's
not wishing me good morning, that's clear. Ruddy cheek. So I shout,
"Speak fucken English."

He stops, swivels on his seat and shouts back, "I speak good English.
Go fuck yourself."

He starts cycling, standing on each pedal in turn, grunting with the
effort. I stride towards him. He's all unawares of the payback coming
his way. I throw a punch at the side of his face and he buckles. Bet he
regrets stopping now. I drag him to the ground. He scrambles on all
fours, but I take one, two, three long strides and stamp down on his rib
cage. Flatten him. I lean over, grab his top with both hands, pull him
over so I can see his face, and land a punch, and another, and another,
and carry on until he isn't resisting. He just takes it. He's moaning real
quiet, and I stroll over to the trailer, nice and easy, take a closer look.

I grab a handful of food waste, go back to the pathetic heap on the ground, prise open his mouth and shove the stuff in. He retches but I force him facedown into the ground, sit on his back, and wait for him to go still. All the while, I'm rehearsing a pep talk for our own migrant workers about showing respect to their betters.

———

I don't slip back into bed with Yana. I take a shower and sit up waiting for everyone to wake. The kids have their breakfast and take themselves off to school after giving me baby bear hugs. As soon as they're out the door, I ask Yana to give me a manicure. Jeez, does she look surprised. I don't smile, so she knows I'm dead serious, and I tell her that I want my nails cleaned and polished up real bright, like fucken fish scales.

PART 3

FOUR YEARS LATER

CHAPTER 8

CALEB

It's a gamble, but it's worth the risk if I reach the fish tanks before anyone else. Sprinting from the dormitory when I'm half-asleep, the night alert still ringing in my ears, I could trip on the cracked ground again. The scabs have only just dropped off from my last fall on the concrete yard. Pink patches on my knees and elbows. Not a good look. Last week broke the record—the alarm rang five nights in a row. Truth is, we need a new technician. Holden takes no pride in his work.

Father's voice pops into my head: "You might as well do a job *properly*, Caleb, as do it *badly*." I don't argue with that, not now, but back then I'd have sulked. I can remember his voice, his words. I can't see his face, but I don't really want to. I swear, he never knew hard work in his life. Not like I fucken know it.

I take a shortcut across the warehouse loading bays. The concrete is badly broken up where the transporters swing around and reverse up. Twice a week we load the transporters with boxes packed with tilapia and ice. We'll be a few boxes short for the deliveries on Saturday if we can't sort out tonight's emergency. I feel bad when there's a cock-up because, when production drops, it's the city wholesalers who come first. The enclave, just a kilometre away, always loses out.

Not that I've been to the enclave. But from the top of the dormitory block, I've seen the edge of the enclave with its workshops and the housing blocks beyond. Easy to imagine it's W3 if I ignore the surrounding woodlands of the Mersey Forest. Probably, this camp is fifty or more kilometres from W3. Maybe a hundred. I'm stupid, really; when I'm on the top of the dormitory block, I find myself looking for Ma Lexie's roof, wondering if Zach or Mikey is now the overseer.

I slow down as I reach the warehouse. The door needs a good shove. I glance across at the control panels. No one's there. An alert is repeating on a cycle of three pings followed by a voice: *Check oxygen levels in tanks seven, eight, nine, ten, eleven and twelve.* I rush towards the raised metal walkway that runs between two rows of tanks, climb the steps and pace the length. The walkway clangs with each step, and the sound echoes across the warehouse. I peer into the green plastic tanks on my left, numbered carelessly in white paint from seven to twelve. I twist around to compare with tanks one to six on my right.

Fish are sucking air at the water surface in the problem tanks, which is bad news, but easy to fix with extra pumping. The real cause is overstocking. Holden is late in separating the bigger fish, and if we don't take action they'll soon start to eat the smaller ones. As problems go, it's not unusual. Nine times out of ten, it's either the temperature and oxygen levels, or a blocked filter, or a pump failure.

Over the years, I've seen so many different problems—and watched how they've been fixed—that I swear I could do Holden's job. He's an enclave resident, and he hates staying at the camp midweek, on call for any emergency. I'm his right-hand man at the fish tanks, even if he doesn't admit it, and I'm surprised he doesn't put me in charge of night calls. I guess he needs the extra pay.

Me, I'd like to spend more time on the salad stacks at the other end of the warehouse—racks and racks, five high in each stack, growing salad leaves and herbs—and all fed by the wastewater from our fish tanks. I help out now and then on the stacks when there's sickness in the camp and they're short staffed. Or if there's a system fail, a die-off, and the racks need replanting. I hope I'll get the transfer soon. That's why I'm making a special effort, racing to sort out all the night-time emergencies, take the credit.

The warehouse door opens and Holden shouts across, "What's the problem?"

I tell him to turn up the aeration pumps. I run down to him. "Should we net some of the bigger fish?"

"Don't bother. Leave it for the morning." He walks off. Panic over as far as he's concerned. If I owned this farm, I'd shift the biggest fish right away.

I don't argue with him because my one goal is to keep my job in aquaponics, either here with the fish, or with the salads. The alternative is shovelling rubbish and ash at the power-from-waste plant at the far side of the camp. Aquaponics is the easiest job for any indentured migrant as long as you know what you're doing, as long as you're smart enough. Half the migrants allocated to aquaponics are booted out within a month. They don't get it, that this isn't a labouring job. There's hard work for sure, but all day, every day, you have to watch the fish—*really* observe them—see how they behave. And on the stacks, you have to observe the salad leaves for any sign of distress.

One day when I'm out of here, with the right-to-remain, I'll start my own business. A small version of this. I've already worked out a plan. I'll need an abandoned building, a few second-hand tanks, plumbing gear and lighting. Plus the day-to-day supplies like fish food and the small tilapia fry. I hope to find a building that's close to other food businesses—their waste will be my fish food. Okay, I'll need more mechanical know-how about fixing the pumps, the biodisks and the like. But I'm picking that up already. I know how the whole process works on our side of the warehouse, from the fish tanks to the settlement and treatment tanks. And that's the important part, because we have to get it right on our side so that our wastewater is perfect for the hydroponics stacks. I've decided I could make a decent living selling fish and salad from even a small operation on a rooftop.

That's how I see this unpaid job: I'm an apprentice. It's the only way I can stop myself from getting hacked off, to pretend the work here is part of my own big plan. I'll be a fish-and-salad king one day.

It's difficult to remember how useless I felt when I arrived here— three years, eight months, two days ago. I kept to myself for a couple of weeks. I watched and made mental notes, listened in on conversations in the canteen. Soon enough I realised I must grab a job at the fish tanks. An older migrant called Javier—Portuguese—gave me a tip-off. At the time, Javier was close to finishing his ten years of indentures, and he showed new arrivals around the camp. I kept close to him, asking questions, and he's the one who told me you had to be smart to work in aquaponics, warned me we'd soon be taking tests.

Apart from winning a job in aquaponics, I also knew I had to hang out with the football crew because they were the toughest. No one hassles you if you're in the first team.

So, it was all about passing tests of one kind or another. An intelligence test for the aquaponics jobs, and a tough trial to join the football team.

I had an advantage over the other migrants because my English was far better. Three Spanish boys asked me to help them with their pronunciation. And I did help. Not as much as I could have done, if I'm honest with myself. I made excuses like I felt sick. No way, I thought. No way was I going to help someone if it meant I lost out. That would be stupid. We took the test—maths, reading and writing in English, puzzles—and I scored the top mark out of thirteen migrants in that month's intake. Three of us were allowed to work with the fish. That's when I knew things were looking up for me. No high hopes—I was still stuck in a shithole. But for the first time since I left Ma Lexie, when she offered me my own label, I felt a bit special, like I was at the beginning of something better.

———

Emergency sorted, I return to the dormitory, and I find a kid in the late-arrivals bunk by the entrance door.

"You okay? Speak English?" I ask.

He shakes his head. "Español," he says.

I lean in real close because we're not allowed to speak any foreign language, only English. I ask him in Spanish how long he's been in the country. He tells me he hasn't been here long. I'm pleased. The only time we hear any news is when there's a new arrival. The best informed are those picked up as soon as they arrive in the country. I tell him I'll see him at breakfast.

I climb back onto my top bunk and lie flat on my back—that way I'll sleep deeply even if it means I'll snore. No one complains about my snoring any longer, not since that Greek kid threw his shoe at me one night. I didn't challenge him the next morning. No, I waited until our kick-around after our shift. I clobbered him in a tackle, knocked him flat. He reckoned I cracked three of his ribs, but I argued it was an accident. Everyone got the message though.

Tonight, I'm not dropping back to sleep so easy. I roll onto my side and straightaway I feel guilty. I find myself thinking about my mother, about how she'd sit on my bed when I felt sick, how she'd stroke my hair.

I told the police and immigration that my parents were both dead. A good son would never do that. It was Jerome who gave me the idea, and I was young then, so he shares the blame. An orphan stood a better chance, he said, and that's all I could think about as I walked away from him and stepped up to the police station entrance. I chose my story and I've stuck to it all this time. It's probably true. Even if my parents are alive, they haven't found me, have they? As good as dead, that's what I tell myself. What's that English saying? Don't split hairs.

When I first said it, that my parents were dead, it felt like the most important moment since I'd left Spain. Because the past became the past. From that moment, I walked into the future. In the interview room, the police officer read my documents, which were creased and water damaged despite all the care I'd taken. She asked if I was hungry. She brought me hot fish and chips from a shop down the street. She sat with me while I ate them, and as soon as I'd finished, she asked all the questions that Jerome had prepared me for. When I'd finished my story, she told me I'd done well, and then she left me on my own. For ages.

She returned looking hard. A deep crease between her eyes. No more smiles. She'd written a statement for me to sign. She said I must listen carefully. Later in the day, an immigration officer would be arriving from the North of England Migrant Reception Centre outside Liverpool. It's a big facility, she said, and it would take time to process my request to stay in England. If my request was approved, I'd be sent to an enclave education and indenture camp outside one of the enclaves. Liverpool usually sent migrants to the one outside Frodsham, she told me. I remember she leaned forward and told me she wouldn't have any more involvement in my application to remain in this country. I remember her next words clearly: "You will only hear from me or my colleagues if we decide to prosecute the man, Jaspar, who held you captive. You'll be called to give evidence in court." I felt like throwing up. And I've had nightmares about that, meeting Jaspar again.

The policewoman—she told me to call her Helen—led me to the police station showers. Told me to have a good scrub, that I should try to make a good impression with the immigration officer. Helen said she couldn't do anything about a change of clothes, because there wasn't time. But she did bring me two meat pies, saying it might be a while before I had a meal at the Liverpool facility. She was right. After those pies, I didn't get anything to eat until the following day.

I lived in a dormitory at the Liverpool facility, like now, and spent four months waiting for something to happen—a decision. I had a weekly interview with Case Officer Farquharson, pronounced Farkuson. Honest, that was a difficult start for any migrant with no English. A warning that English wasn't easy. The surprising thing about Farquharson was how scruffy she looked, with her hair all over the place and a cardigan with stains. She looked more like a migrant than the migrants. She organised all my medical checks including the DNA test. The worst part was the dental check. I didn't even have toothache, but the dentist took out three teeth, telling me it was better to take them out early than suffer pain in the future. And I learned later that the indenture camp didn't get many dental visits. So, I guess it was a good idea to have the three teeth taken out.

All that time in the Liverpool facility, I didn't say anything in my interviews about Ma Lexie because I worried that any information about Ma Lexie could link me with the block of flats across the street, and with Odette. I'd convinced myself that Odette had murdered her janitor. Or at least, Odette *left* her for dead. Instead, I told Farquharson exactly what I told the police, that I worked in Jaspar's recycling yard. Truth is, I'd only seen Jaspar a couple of times when he came to the roof to see Ma Lexie, but I saw enough to describe him. I told Farquharson I couldn't describe the person who trafficked me to Jaspar because everything happened at night-time. It didn't feel right shopping Skylark. I don't know why. So I only told the policewoman and Farquharson about Skylark's jacket with the feathers.

Looking back, those months in Liverpool blur into one repeated day. I tried to avoid talking to other people. The more I talked, I decided, the more chance I had of saying something careless. I was sure some of the migrants were reporting on one another. And all the time I expected news to break. I worried that Odette would be caught, and she might say I'd helped her escape, that I knew she planned to attack her boss. Even if she had good reasons for murdering her boss, I didn't want the finger pointing at me.

Officer Farquharson never came back to me to say they'd found a DNA match. I hoped every time I saw her that she'd have news, but then I felt relieved when she didn't. I didn't know *what* I wanted. What made me angry, and still does, is that Mother didn't do her homework. If we'd arrived together at a reception centre, we'd have been shipped straight back to Spain, like Jerome said.

In one big way, the Liverpool centre was better than here. There were girls. Our dormitories, canteens and recreation rooms were separate, but we mixed together outdoors. That's why, even as winter started, we stayed outside until the last second of outdoor rec. And even though I played shy—because girls make better spies than boys—we all had a laugh together, and one of the Italian girls started to hang out with me, like she fancied me. But I didn't dare trust her.

Arriving here, discovering the indenture camp was male only, that was a shock. Families were split up, and I felt pleased it didn't affect me. Fights broke out over nothing. Lots of anger and no way to burn it off. But the guards came down heavy—shock prods, isolation cells, chemical sleeps—and that's probably why we have escape attempts among the new arrivals, and from time to time a suicide. I wish they'd wait, give the place a chance. I swear to God, what really annoys me is when an older migrant commits suicide, because that's setting a real bad example.

I'm not as angry as I used to be about anything really, and I think the inoculation has properly kicked in. We talk about it, us indentured labourers, because we can all tell the difference, some more than others. I think it explains why we tend to settle in eventually. The inoculations are given to most migrants, but I don't know how it's decided. No one explains. But since I'm from Spain, and European law bans the inoculations, I was jabbed straight off, and now I'm feeling different. Like Skylark warned me: "You won't be the same afterwards. You'll lose your spark."

I'm not sure I mind. I do feel calmer most of the time, and I sleep better. Skylark exaggerated, whereas Mother always spoke in favour. She said, "Why would they put up with troublemakers?" Or something like that. Javier says he feels free, which is a mad thing to say. He says he doesn't care any more, doesn't miss his drinking.

Anyway, it's done, and I'm due for a booster.

———

I push my way through the queue for breakfast, stand next to the new kid. He follows my lead: takes the porridge, milk and eggs. I lead him to a table as far away as possible from the guard because I'll have to speak in Spanish to the kid. I give the nod to two of my football mates, and they do the same to two more. They join us at our table before anyone else can take the seats. While the canteen staff are making a din serving food, I ask questions in a low voice and pass on the news from the kid, as short bulletins, headlines: More migrants are trying to cross the Channel than last year. The weather is hotter. No rain for two months. France has brought in a new law—full life imprisonment for starting a wildfire. Portugal is talking about execution for arson. We all grunt our approval. My mate, the fullback, says, "The fuckers deserve chopping down."

A loud buzzer. We stand immediately. Time for class and we begin to file out. I put my hand on the new kid's shoulder. Everyone needs a show of kindness when they first arrive, but a pat on the shoulder is as far as it goes. He'll have to toughen up fast.

As we make our way to class, I think back to my days back home. I had no idea what was going on in the world. Too young to care or understand. Until I left Spain, all I thought about was finishing my schoolwork and escaping the flat as soon as possible to play football. I didn't even realise the water shortages were serious until my parents stopped washing our clothes. True, I had to stand for hours in the water queue, swapping places with my mother or father, but my friends did the same. Standing in queues was normal—for everyone.

Now that I'm older, though, I do ask myself why my parents didn't act quicker. They followed the news. We should have left sooner as a family, when I was a baby or before I started school, when it was easier to cross borders, when we didn't need visas.

That's what parents are supposed to do. Think ahead and protect their kids.

———

Mr. Tuckwell barks, "Scrambled egg on toast. Scrambled egg on toast. After me: Scrambled egg on toast."

A spot check on an old vocabulary list, with a new teacher. Half the class struggles with his accent. The way he says "toast," he sounds like a foghorn. He's from Lancashire. Truth is, I don't think he's a proper teacher. This isn't how I learned English back in Spain. All he does is talk, and if we don't understand, he talks louder. Sometimes I wonder if all the hopeless teachers are sent to teach in the camps. Because a good teacher would refuse to work in such a miserable classroom with so many students. If you sit at the back, you can hardly hear. No pictures on the walls. One window facing the fish farm has been cracked since I arrived here, and half the glass fell out last winter. Never fixed. Once the cold weather starts, no one will want to sit near it.

Sweat trickles down the back of Javier's neck. He sits on the bench in front of me. He's nearly thirty, and he's worked his indentures for fourteen years now. He can't pass the English tests, spoken or written. I think his hearing isn't great, which can't help, so maybe he'll never get out of here.

English lessons, five days a week, one hour straight after breakfast. A year after I arrived, admin posted a new rule: *Speaking in a language other than English will be punished by an extension in the offender's indenture term.* They brought in that rule overnight. Stress levels hit the roof. But me, I was glad. I hated that thing when a bunch of kids, men, too, stared at you from across the canteen, talked in their own language and laughed loud. A total wind-up. You knew they were having a joke at your expense. That sort of thing led to fights, but I never let it get to me. I sort out my frustrations on the football pitch.

"Come on then. What else? What else do we eat for breakfast? You!" He's looking straight at me. "Porridge with cold milk, Mr. Tuckwell."

"After me, everyone. Porridge with cold milk. Porridge with cold milk."

Tuckwell likes us to reply with more than one word. He likes phrases and whole sentences. A single-word reply earns you a clip.

I don't complain to anyone. English is easy for me. It's the weekend culture classes I hate. We're supposed to have one full day's rest at the weekend, but culture class eats into our day off by two whole hours. Most of it's stupid. Like, I learned that English people think the Spanish are rude because we don't say "please" or "thank you" often enough. We have to memorise all the kings and queens of England—and all the wars they won. Mr. Hannah, our latest culture instructor, says that if we want to live here peacefully and succeed in life, we have to learn from history and leave behind old-fashioned religions and superstitions. He says that this is a modern world, and we must all strive to be modern people. That's the way we will live together peacefully on this small island. That sounds right to me. I don't get religion anyway.

It's funny though that Mr. Hannah doesn't like religion, yet he has us chant the ten rules of the camp, like the Ten Commandments. That makes me laugh inside, but I can't smile. If I'm caught on the classroom cameras, that kind of *bad attitude* earns a caning. Every lesson starts with a song, the same one, "Jerusalem." We all shout the lyrics and by the end of the song, I feel stirred up, but relaxed at the same time, like I've emptied myself of all my frustrations, and I shout loudest near the end of the song—"I will not cease from mental fight, nor shall my sword sleep in my hand." At the end of every lesson, we sing "God Save the King." It's so slow and miserable that I leave the classroom feeling down.

———

Tanks seven to twelve are sorted. It took half an hour with a team of four to separate the bigger fish. While we're doing the hard work, the nutrients' supplier shows up in the warehouse, and he and Holden slip out together. They'll be doing a deal, and we all pretend we don't know what's going on. Truth is, I saw Holden packing a few of the big tilapia that we'd netted. I expect those will be changing hands right now. Maybe that's the modern man's way of doing business.

With the stock tanks running normally, with no fish gasping for oxygen, I check the sedimentation tank, which sits between our operation and the salad stacks. The wastewater from our fish tanks flows through this tank, where the fish poo settles out. Sounds disgusting but this liquid is full of nutrients, so it's perfect for hydroponics.

While no one's looking, I push through the black industrial curtains into the salad lines, lit up so bright. Peppers, salad leaves, herbs, all growing with their roots dangling in long shallow trays, fed with our wastewater. I love it in here. And it's easier work. If I could get a full-time transfer into here, instead of doing the odd day, I'd understand the whole process.

"Oy! What are you doing in here?" I turn to see Holden. "You're wanted. In the admin block at one o'clock. After midday break."

He's taking the piss. Midday break. It's first-come, first-served when sandwiches are brought to the warehouse. Midday means any time they feel like dishing up. If you're the last to get there, then you're likely to find every last sandwich gone. I reckon the fish are better fed than we are.

So, I'm wanted in admin, and I'm wondering if a lucky break is coming my way. I'm due one because I set things up with the salad technician. I wanted a transfer to his section, and he promised to put in a good word for me, but only after I gave him the silver locket I stole at the vineyard. Immigration let me keep it because I said it belonged to my mother. It helped that I'd cut up the photo of my father and slid the image of his face into the locket. And all these years, I'd held on to it for something important. Honest to God, I hated the sight of the locket, knowing I stole it from a dead woman.

It's now three months since the salad technician said he'd request my transfer. But I'm not convinced I can trust him. Suspect he fobbed me off. Still, if he did put in the request, then this could be it.

————

No sign of the sandwiches, and it's time to go. I ask Holden for permission to leave, and he tells me not to waste any time getting back because there's masses to do before the deliveries tomorrow. I feel like telling him: If he made a flea-sized effort himself we'd have no problem. Just like Mr. Ben at Ma Lexie's. How does it happen? How do the lazy bastards get these jobs? Or did they work hard only until they got promotion? Like the promotion is the endgame.

The admin blocks are all single storey. Most of them were thrown up as the camp expanded with each wave of migrants. The site looks as if a child has tossed building bricks across the ground. The first blocks, brightly coloured at one time, have faded in the sun. The newer ones are all shades of grubby grey; no one's pretending this is a fun place to spend a few years.

The steel door to the labour administration block has been repainted blue since I last reported here. The maintenance crew didn't bother to paint the words "Labour Administration" in a different colour, but I can see the shape of the letters underneath, despite the paint runs. This is the office for us labourers, and it's tucked away at the scruffiest end of the admin blocks. I tug open the door. It scrapes across the concrete, and I'm reminded of the night on Ma Lexie's roof. Takes me right back to that moment when I carefully eased open the roof door, trying not to wake her or the boys. It seems a long time ago, and I wish I could turn back the clock, close that door and stay there on the roof. But I have to keep going forward and show everyone I want to make a success of myself. Today could be a big step in the right direction.

A camp auxiliary sits at a grey metal desk with a dent in its side panel. He looks up. I tell him I've been told to report here, and he tells me to sit and wait. The walls are bare, the bench hard and the floor gritty. Two minutes later an alert on his screen catches his attention. "Room Seven," he tells me.

Before today, I'd reported to Room Three, which is the labour superintendent's office where new work assignments are handed out. I take slow steps towards Room Seven, trying to imagine what I'm here for if it isn't about my work reassignment to the salad line. It can't be an interrogation, because they happen on the opposite side of the camp in a brick building next to the isolation wing. So, what's this all about? Should I knock?

I *do* knock, twice, and wait. After a couple of seconds: "Come in." A woman's voice? I push open the door but I don't step in.

"Hello, Caleb. Come in. I am Executive Officer Sonia."

I enter the room. Who the hell is she? All neat and tidy, but no uniform.

"You can call me Officer Sonia." She smiles. "Take a seat. Now, it states here, Caleb, that you have a good command of English, but do tell me if I use a word you don't understand."

I bump into the chair, fall into it rather than sitting down, and the chair shifts on the floor. I straighten up but the chair doesn't sit flat—one leg is short.

"You do look much older now." She shows me her screen: a photo of me taken at the Liverpool Reception Centre just before, or just after, my thirteenth birthday. She's from immigration?

"Don't look so worried, Caleb. I've checked your case notes, and I'm here today to revisit the statements you made at the time you handed yourself in. That was a very intelligent decision, wasn't it?"

She looks down as though I'm not required to speak.

My hands are sweating.

"No regrets, I assume," she says. "About surrendering?"

My ears are ringing, and the room side shifts like I might pass out. I shake my head.

She raises her eyebrows at me. "It's just paperwork."

"Is it about . . . ?"

"What, Caleb?"

"Jaspar. Is there a court case? Because it's a long time ago. I'm not sure I'd remember—"

"Nothing to do with Jaspar." She looks at her screen. "Let's see . . . Jaspar. Ah, here. No court case." She swipes. "Your word against his in the end. No corroborating evidence." The soles of my feet are sparking. The total relief! If there's one bad dream that won't go away, it's me meeting Jaspar, and him chasing me.

"I'm looking into a number of anomalies, of which you are one, Caleb. You have done nothing wrong as such. Your original case officer, Farquharson, is no longer working in the immigration service. I'm going through her case files. And while I'm here at the camp, I'll be talking with your instructors to check if you've adjusted well during the past four years and if you show promise. We have other schemes for migrants who struggle to adapt, migrants who are unlikely to assimilate within the general population. But the indications from your annual updates are good. So let's get started on these original statements, shall we?"

I don't trust her. Why do my old statements need checking? The process is simple. Finish indentures, pass the English and culture tests. And with my right-to-remain status, I'll walk out of this place, get a job on the outside, or start a business. Unless there's a rule change coming. Are they increasing the number of years we have to serve indentures? It's happened before. Javier told me so.

For the next hour, I'm forced by this woman, Officer Sonia, to dig into my memories, and it isn't easy. My head is pounding. I'm terrified of mixing up fact and fiction. They were separated in my mind four years ago, but I haven't had any warning, and if I'd known this was going to happen, I'd have rehearsed my story as I did with Jerome under the bridge. She goes through my entire history: the journey with my mother through France; how I crossed the English Channel; how I ended up working for Jaspar at the recycling yard; how I escaped. Why did I walk to the vineyards? How did I find my way there? Did someone tell me the vineyards were a good place to hide out? She wanted to know how I avoided being picked up in the vineyard immigration raid. I told her it was luck. I happened to be filling a wine jug at the far side of the courtyard.

"I'd like a drink of water," I say.

"This won't take long."

She doesn't give me a moment to get myself together, get my head straight. We're back to the earlier part of the story. Is my father still in Spain? How could I be *sure* he set off for England in the first place? What proof did I have that my father was dead?

How am *I* supposed to have proof? I was a kid back then. I don't understand. Why is she going into all this? I've been in the camp all these years. She stands up and, without speaking, leaves the room.

Thank God. Slow, deep breaths, but it doesn't calm me. I'm thinking about how the interrogation began—because this isn't a conversation, she's after something. Or she's provoking me into losing my temper. Then my indentures will be extended for bad behaviour. They want to keep me here longer? That can't be it. New arrivals have increased this summer. Is there a chance I'll be released early? Is she making sure I'm suitable for early release? Could that be it?

The door opens. She places a cup of water on the desk and pushes it towards me. I'm so thirsty I down it in one, and as I place the cup on the table, she stares at me, frowning. I feel my blood drain right out, and, I swear, I see a big, dark pool on the floor.

She says, "In your statement you said your mother had died. But you don't know that for sure, do you? It's a calculated guess. Yes?"

She backtracks, goes over and over my story, the same questions, and I've no clue why she talked about my mother that way. I think she's bluffing, testing my story to the limit. One question after another like a dog that won't stop barking.

Silence, at last, and I feel I've been in a punch-up with no bruises to show for a solid beating. She sighs heavily. She's disappointed in me. I look past her, through the window. A single tiny cloud in a blue sky.

"Please look at me, Caleb. Did you actually see your mother's body in the ditch as it says here in your statement? I am offering you the opportunity to set the record straight."

I've had enough. I tell her that my mother must be dead because she'd lost her mind and walked off in the night without any warm clothes, and she hadn't come back. "I waited over a week for her. She must have died."

"So, you didn't find her body. Thank you, Caleb. I dislike loose ends. And with that particular one tied up, I can show you this . . ."

She turns her screen to me, but I don't recognise the woman in the image, not straightaway. Short grey hair. A face full of dirty wrinkles. Cheeks sagging, like she hasn't smiled in a long time. But she's my mother. I reach with fingertips, and, as I stroke the deep creases by her eye, it all hits me at once. I feel a jolt and I'm on my feet. My chair crashes back against the floor.

Officer Sonia says, "I'm pleased to inform you that your mother is alive."

"Where . . . ?"

"There's no harm in telling you. She's in a psychiatric wing at a migrant detention facility in the south of England."

"Where, where?" I can hardly get the words out. "Exactly where?"

"Dover. But you don't need to concern yourself with that. The fact is, Caleb, your mother may have been confused when she left your tent in the night, but she didn't die. A victim of trafficking. We picked her up in a raid. She had no documentation, and she remains in a very confused state of mind. She hasn't told us her name or where she's from."

"You mean she's sick. Really sick?"

"Yes. But the puzzle over her identity is now solved. Her DNA matches yours. So, the immigration service has decided it's your responsibility to bring her back to good health. We'll reunite you as soon as logistically possible. I had arranged for your transfer this afternoon, but the transport appears to be double-booked. We'll rearrange as soon as possible."

"What about my father?"

"No information."

I'm winded. Reunited? Now? Halfway through indentures? Jerome's warning comes flooding back: it's easier to stay in the country if your parents are dead. That's it. They'll reunite and deport us.

———

I don't know how I manage it, but I stand and walk out of the room. I've no idea how long she's been questioning me. When I arrive back

at the warehouse, I take a bollocking from Holden. I don't hear a word
he says. Three hours I've been gone and I can't speak, can't even say *I'm
sorry* to Holden. He carries on raging, trying to get some reaction.

The other labourers are shitty with me, too, when I join them in the
tilapia packing bay. Take a few shoulder barges, as in *The fuck you been,
pal?* I could say, "Guess what, guys? My mother's alive."

What the hell?

I feel bad I didn't know her face. It took a few seconds. And I know
I shouldn't think it, but it's obvious—she's a different person now. I'm
wrong to feel angry, but I can't help it. I've gone through all this shit
on my own, slaving away, lost all my friends, and none of it's my fault.
Look at the total fucken mess she and Father kicked off.

But, still, I could see her. Just about. Behind those eyes, somewhere.

I keep my mouth shut, take the elbow digs, and I work on auto:
fish, ice, box, fish, ice, box.

CHAPTER 9

OFFICER SONIA

Not a single hair out of place. The side parting in Superintendent Guidy's jet-black hair is exactly straight. I imagine him standing in front of his bathroom mirror this very morning. He slicks back his hair and executes the division well off-centre. With comb and palm, he sweeps his hair from one side of the parting, then sweeps from the other side. Not a single speck of lint on his dark, deep-blue suit. It fits his large frame perfectly. He dresses as though he's the manager of a six-star hotel rather than the superintendent of an unstarred migrant education and indenture camp.

I devote barely a second's thought, any day of the week, to my appearance, my clothing. It's all arranged for me. Standard-issue attire: one work suit and five shirts, laundered by housekeeping at the rest station and delivered to my room on Sunday evening. Two sets of casual clothing. We all wear the same. It saves so much time. But, of course, I've no need to impress anyone by the way I look. No one ever questions my abilities. I dress plainly. I deliver results without fail.

Unlike Farquharson.

"My technicians won't be happy," says Superintendent Guidy. He slumps down in his chair, his suit now rucking up above his shoulders.

"The kid's made himself useful." And half-heartedly: "Can't you turn a blind—?"

I raise my left palm to him. "Superintendent, we must right this wrong. The solution to institutional corruption is not *more* institutional corruption."

"That's a bit strong," he says.

"Farquharson sent eight migrants—who ought to have been deported—to various indenture camps. Caleb should never have entered this camp."

"She made a few mistakes. That isn't corruption as I know it. No money changed hands," he says.

"Not in a literal sense. Farquharson's mistakes, as you call them, all took place during the last six weeks of her appraisal period. Those eight *mistakes* allowed her to meet her targets for admissions to migrant education and indenture camps. And thus, she received a bonus."

"Hold on, that's not the same as a backhander."

Do I really need to explain? Much as I appreciate leaving the office, it is tiresome dealing with such muddled thinking.

"Surely you can see, Superintendent, there's a substantial cost to the public purse. Farquharson, in her role as a first-contact case officer, logged Caleb into the system in Liverpool and almost immediately received notification of a DNA match. She buried that information. Caleb's mother had already been detained as the result of an immigration swoop, but we could not deport her because she didn't have documentation and didn't even know her own name. If we'd paired them up, and with Caleb's birth certificate and so on, we'd have deported them to Spain forthwith. Instead, Farquharson won her bonus—one cost to the state. Caleb came *here*, and that's another cost regardless of his indentured work. In addition, look at the cost of accommodating his mother in a psychiatric wing. Farquharson's actions are indefensible."

I stand, ready to take my leave, but Superintendent Guidy doesn't budge. I don't think he's ready to acquiesce.

He says, "The trouble is, you see, it's difficult to cope with all these targets because the priorities shift from one day to the next. Don't get me wrong, I don't condone Farquharson's actions, but I can sympathise." Oh dear, he thinks his experience will sway me. "Look at my situation," he says. "One year I'm told to retain as many migrants as possible; the next year I'm told to push them out."

"Supply and demand. We can't take a static position."

"I prefer things more clear-cut, Sonia."

I smooth the creases from my jacket. Why does it . . . rankle, or is *that* too strong? I must address him as superintendent, but *he* may call me Sonia. And now I wonder, seeing as Superintendent Guidy "prefers things clear-cut," maybe the entire immigration process, the whole *shebang*—I like that word—should be delegated to us simulants. Be done with it! People with brain chips imagine they're one rung down on the IQ ladder from us. They're way below, closer to organics than to us. And it may seem counterintuitive, but I find that my interpersonal relationships are far more straightforward with organics.

"One thing is perfectly clear," I say. "No matter how handy this boy, Caleb, has proved to be, Superintendent, we both know the place won't fall apart for the sake of one indentured labourer. Plenty more where he came from, especially now with the resurgence of drought and wildfires in southern Europe."

"Makes you bloody wonder, doesn't it? Are there any trees left to burn?"

I let that hang in the air. Allow myself a discreet eye roll.

He says, "We thought we'd seen the worst of the wildfires, and here we go again."

Better to leave him on a good note. "You have to admit, Superintendent, that immigration has succeeded in transforming a negative into a positive. Look how your camp has expanded over the past fifteen years, and how you've taken those basic fish farms and moved into large-scale aquaponics. They play such an important role in food supply. So, feel proud."

He sits up. "I do. And, I'll have you know, Sonia, I've achieved more. The department acted on my advice regarding the revised conditions for right-to-remain. I told them: make simple, minor adjustments. And that's what they did—gradually toughening the tests for spoken and written English. Let's face it, no one could object to that, could they? New punishment tariffs, too, so that rule infringements incurred significant extensions in the period of indenture service. We were smart about it, don't you think? No single change rang alarms for the bleeding hearts here or abroad."

I'm nodding, but I wrap things up. "Have the boy ready. I'll reschedule the transport pickup—I hope for tomorrow."

The overhead lights flicker along the corridor. I'll sleep easier tonight, knowing I've made a start on Farquharson's aberrant case files. Not that I'm anxious. I feel a sense of repulsion as if—what's that idiom?—I'm washing someone else's soiled linen. She had to be sacked, though I recognise her impulse wasn't entirely self-serving. She wished to provide better for her daughter, to take her on holiday, to visit family in Scotland. And Farquharson isn't the only one deviating from the approved process. I've sifted ten years of case files at the Liverpool Reception Centre, cross-checked the communication streams with other agencies, flagged when data has been incorrectly assigned, pinpointed incorrect decisions, those at odds with legislation and guidelines.

I smile to myself. When I undertook my orientation programme with the immigration service, I made an observation that fell on stony ground. I suggested that the costs to the state of an open-door policy would be less than the present costs of the state's immigration control apparatus. My supervisor informed me that direct costs and direct benefits did not reflect the full economic picture. He'd no idea that I *had* considered the full picture.

I'm opening the door of my small transporter when Superintendent Guidy calls across from the office entrance. He walks gingerly towards me. "Fancy a nice fish salad for dinner? I'll get one of the boys to prep some fillets. I'll pack them in ice. And a salad selection too. Follow me!"

"Wait. I don't cook. Never have. I don't have a kitchen." I fall in behind him, trying to explain. "We dine in a canteen, Superintendent."

He's striding off. "Come and take a look."

———

I don't have a keen sense of smell, but I can certainly smell fish!

"It doesn't smell like this all the time," he says, reading my mind. "They're packing the cold boxes for tomorrow's deliveries."

His technician spots us, wanders over. Superintendent Guidy asks him, "How about a tilapia takeaway for our visitor?"

A familiar request no doubt. The man doesn't blink. "No problem." He turns to me. "Salad box too?"

I nod, attempt a smile. "Thank you."

Why explain? I'll simply hand over the fish and salad to the canteen boss. I watch the technician shoulder into the packing line, lean over to pull out enough tilapia to feed both sittings at the C6 Rest Station. All the labourers look identical in their overalls and boots, but I catch sight of Caleb. He must sense my eyes on him because he throws a backwards glance. His face is pale. Ashen. Now that I reflect on it, he wasn't joyous at the news of his mother's discovery. I didn't focus on his lack of reaction at the time, as my priority was to complete, without delay, the next steps—organising transport, booking their passage to Santander.

I actually felt relieved for Caleb, that he'd escape this dead-end job. All told, was it really worth the trek to England for this? Surely he's better off with his mother. Start afresh back home. It's not as though he's seeking asylum. His life isn't in danger.

As the technician hands over the cold box to the superintendent, I ask by way of small talk, "Do these workers give you any trouble?"

"When they first arrive. Takes about six months for the inoculations to kick in, but then they're okay."

"What about the boy, Caleb?"

"Good worker."

"Anything else . . . ?"

"What's there to say? They come, they go. Some work better than others."

"I want to speak to him again. Bring him over."

Caleb drags himself like a sullen child across the warehouse, comes to a halt a little too far from me. I wave him forward. I turn to the superintendent. "Leave me with him."

He shrugs and moves out of earshot.

"What's the matter with you, Caleb? Why aren't you happy with the news? You and your mother can start over, even if your father is still missing."

"He's dead."

"But you and your mother? What about that?"

He glances over his shoulder at the packing line, then back at me. "I didn't recognise her."

"There's no mistake."

"She looks sick. It's a shock."

"A good one though."

He's downcast, a child again, clamming up. I wait him out. He looks up with tears in his eyes, wipes his nose with the back of his hand and says, "I don't think she'll know me."

The technician walks towards us with an overfilled salad box. I say to Caleb, "Of course she'll know you. You'll see her soon. Now, off you go, back to work."

As he joins the packing line, he's jostled by workers on either side. You'd think they'd stick together, support one another, wouldn't you?

The superintendent and I carry the boxes out of the warehouse. He says, "No second thoughts about the kid?"

Is he trying to bribe me with fish? Surely not. "Look, Superintendent Guidy, I accept that Caleb might be an asset. He's a smart boy. But we've known that all along."

"All along?"

"Yes, he came into contact with one of our undercover agents, according to the case notes. Soon after that contact, Caleb handed himself in because the agent convinced him that surrendering was the smart thing to do."

The superintendent nods his approval. "Undercover agent, you say? More exciting than our jobs."

"Not as safe though." I tell him that the undercover agent ran into trouble—badly injured in a mugging. In my opinion, it resulted from his own reckless behaviour. The agent, I explain, followed up on Caleb's story by visiting one of the enclaves outside Manchester, intending to build a case against the boy's incarcerator. It came to nothing, I tell the superintendent, because the agent couldn't uncover any corroborating evidence. "He shouldn't have gone there in the first place without submitting a risk assessment," I add.

"They run on pure adrenaline, those undercover types," says the superintendent. "Who mugged him?"

"We don't know. A random attack."

"So . . . ?"

"He left the service. Went back to the legal world. Tried to sue us for compensation, without success."

We shake hands.

In the vehicle, I pass the journey reading recipes for tilapia, a surprisingly versatile fish it seems, pairing with most seasonings. I forward the recipes to the canteen boss at my rest station.

CHAPTER 10

CALEB

What the hell did Officer Sonia want? She expected me to jump up and down, hug her? Wanted me to shout, *She's alive! She's alive!* I was too shocked.

Does she want tears of happiness now, when I'm still numb? I stare at the concrete floor of the warehouse, at a puddle of water that reflects the overhead lighting gantry. I can't switch on tears, but there's one memory that gets to me.

I bring her back. We're side-by-side, working together as a medic team. My last clear memory of Mother acting her normal self, being totally in charge, giving me careful instructions. I see my hand, gripping a white metal cup. I'm pouring salty water on a deep, ragged wound. She speaks so quietly. "Nicely done, Caleb," she says, even though some of the salty water misses the wound. She touches my hand and stops the shaking.

When I look up at Officer Sonia, my eyes are teary. She studies my face and waves me away.

I'm back on the tilapia packing line. The work, repetitive, is steadying my mind a little. With one hand I grab the tail. My other hand takes the weight. With each movement, I'm asking myself, *what now?*

I drift into a daydream. It's a daydream I repeat most days, and it always starts as I imagine a voice asking, "Have you heard about Caleb?" In this daydream, I return home and meet my friend Leo. We hug one another. He steps back, looks me up and down. He laughs in surprise that I've done so well for myself. I'm rich. It's a simple dream, but I have a bigger dream now, for I've rescued my mother. I've rescued her from the psych wing of the Dover Detention Centre. No, wait . . . it's easier to imagine something else . . . My mother is sent to a hospital in Spain while I've stayed in England to make my fortune. And with my fortune made, I've tracked her down. I skip over the details, because you can in a dream. This is what I see: My mother is living in our old home with her own nurse, while I live in a big house nearby. And even though water is still in short supply, let's face it, a rich person can survive anywhere. Whatever the shortages, they spend their way out of all their problems.

The dream tells me it's too soon to go back home.

———

In the canteen I spot Javier and head over to him, but my legs are stiff. I froze solid when Officer Sonia told me about Mother, and I can't thaw out. I sit opposite Javier. He's leaning over his plate, spooning food into his mouth like he's never lifted anything so heavy.

"Hey, bad day?" I ask.

He grunts. "No new arrivals. Shovel rubbish at incinerator. All fucken day."

Before I start to eat, I say, "Javier, tell me about those buildings, the ones you lived in with those other people." I speak slowly and watch his face to see if he understands. "Y'know, when you were caught by immigration."

He looks up. "Why?"

"Thinking ahead. When I get out of here, I want to find an old building, an empty one, abandoned. Set up my own fish tanks and go into business. Understand?"

Under his breath, a long slow "Whoa." He puts down his spoon. He almost laughs, more like a gargle. "Big ideas, man. Give me a job?"

Ignoring his sarcasm, I play it straight. "Sure thing, Javier. So, how did you survive? Where did you find food? Because I'll need time to get the operation up and running."

"Thieving. From gardens, houses."

"You were caught breaking in?"

"Not me. Another guy. Police followed and found us all. Too many migrants in one building. Big problem."

"It's safer to go it alone. Is that what you're saying?"

He nods, goes back to his food.

———

Looking up at the ceiling from my bunk, I admit the truth to myself. Forgot my own rule, didn't I? Be prepared. Over the last few years, all I've thought about is finishing my indentures. I'm not ready to do a runner. When I first arrived here, it was different. I thought night and day about how to escape because the camp was far worse than I expected. Skylark was right. Jerome was wrong. He made indentures sound like the sensible thing to do. But there's never enough food. It's baking hot in the summer, freezing cold in the winter, and we can't leave the camp. I spent one week on starvation rations because I swore in Spanish on the football pitch. No one told me it was a prison.

Old escape plans. Yeah, I thought about escaping with the vehicles leaving the camp—the rubbish trailers leaving the power-from-waste plant, or the transporters from the aquaponics warehouse. I can't remember when exactly, but I lost the hunger to do that. Probably around the time I set myself a new goal, to become the best labourer at the fish tanks.

I've no stash of food, no extra clothes, no torch, no nothing.

I swear, the one and only chance is tomorrow morning. Even then I might be too late if I'm taken away first thing. My breath shivers inside my chest. I close my eyes and concentrate. I have one advantage that I didn't have when I first arrived: I know how to create a diversion. Too bad I don't have time for a practice run.

———

Six of us carry tilapia boxes from the warehouse to the loading bays. Back and forth. I'm hot already—I've kept my sweatpants on under my overalls. Holden stands by the first transporter. He doesn't lift a finger to help. We stack the boxes inside, and I try to drag my feet, slow things down, but it's impossible. We do this job week in and week out. We're on automatic. With the last six boxes loaded, Holden slams the rear doors and sets the destination: this one is heading for the Liverpool wholesale market, and it's packed with the biggest tilapia. Two more transporters need to be packed—one for the Manchester market, and a smaller one for W2, the nearby enclave.

It's all about timing. We load the Manchester transporter, and Holden sets the destination. Off it goes, through the inner and outer gates, with little interest shown by the guard. When the smallest transporter is half-filled, with boxes stacked floor to roof, we trail back to the warehouse. I hang back. The others pick up more boxes and are returning to the loading area when I lay my hands on my next box, as if to lift it up. They're out of sight. I run to the aquaponics control panel and switch off the main aeration pump.

I reappear in the loading area, add my box to the top of the pile.

"Get a fucken move on," says Holden.

"Stone in my boot," I mumble.

We load another twenty-four boxes between us. I'm sweating, and I get the whole frozen-legs thing again when the alarm rings inside the warehouse. We all stop and look at Holden.

"What the hell?" he says. He charges back inside and we all follow, me hanging back again. When they all disappear inside the warehouse, I twist around, hotfoot to the transporter, open the side door. I lift out half a stack of boxes—it's all I can manage—and take them to the rear, push them inside. Return to the side door, climb in, and close the door behind me. I crouch there—there's no room to stand—and I ask myself: What do I have to lose? What's the worst that can happen? If I'm found, I'll be beaten up and then deported with my mother. And all the years I've spent in England will be wasted. All totally pointless.

"Hurry up. Load those and that'll do." Holden's pissed off.

The back doors slam closed. The transporter silently moves away from the loading area. I place my hands on the stacks to the side and front to steady myself. Even so, I lurch as the vehicle stops between the automated inner and outer gates. Another lurch. The outer gates have surely opened. Am I out? Yes, I'm out.

Why didn't I do this before?

I tap my head against the boxes. Father would kill me for this. I feel shame for the first time. It burns me. But it's not fair. It's not my shame, it's my father's. Father was the one who fucked up. I'd tell him straight if I ever saw him again: *You fucked up. Why did you leave without us? Why did you ever believe that was a good idea? Why didn't we all leave years earlier?*

I *know* Mother wouldn't recognise me. There's no point being reunited. Her eyes were dead. She's not the same person. She's not my mother.

In her right mind, she'd want me to take this chance. I believe that. I've no doubt.

I hear sounds. Other vehicles. Stop-start for two or three minutes. Does Holden know I'm missing? He always skives off after we've loaded. With luck he won't notice until after I've reached the enclave.

Is W2 the same as Ma Lexie's enclave? The same street patterns? I'll be ready to run when the transporter's door locks are released. How far have I travelled now? Damn. I should have counted the seconds, the minutes. It occurs to me, the last time I made a real quick decision, when I ran off with Odette, that was a giant mistake. I groan.

The transporter stops and reverses. This must be it. Voices . . . someone calls, "Oy! Over here." I hear the locks release. The back doors open. Shafts of light between the stacked boxes. Too soon to run. Wait. Wait for them to get busy. Minutes seem to pass.

A male voice again. "Oy! Come on!"

Another voice. "Hold your bob hat on." Laughter.

Now. Before anyone climbs inside. While they're fooling around.

I can't feel my feet. They're numb with pins and needles, but I open the door and climb down. The open rear door shields me from the labourers at the back. I'm near blinded by the morning sun, and I start walking, fearing I might fall before my legs find their strength. No time to work out where I am.

Side glances: other vehicles, porters with trolleys, rough ground. Keep my head down. Head for the edge of whatever this is. I don't look back. I spot a group of porters, squatting like they're playing cards. All eyes on the ground between them. I see a shirt thrown over a trolley. I nick it as I stride past because I need to get out of these camp overalls and cover up my camp T-shirt. No one shouts, and I head straight for a street leading off from this open area. I guess the market square is somewhere close by.

It all comes flooding back. The streets just wide enough for two rubbish trailers to scrape past one another. Narrow alleys leading off. I look up to the top of the building. The same. Four floors. Shutters, some open, most of the higher ones closed against the sun. Rooftop activity on both sides of the street, but from this angle I can't tell what those activities are. I take a sharp right into the entrance to a housing block. A concrete stairway faces me. I can't hear anyone. I struggle out of my boots and overalls, pull on the shirt. Boots back on. Chuck the overalls to the back of the hallway, under the stairs.

I'd be an idiot to hope for the best. Always assume the worst. Holden knows I've escaped; he knows I hid in the transporter, that I'm somewhere in the enclave. The alarm has already been rung, word has gone out to the local police—and to immigration. To Officer Sonia. I must hide until dark and then head off to the forests on the distant hills. Keep off the roads. I won't risk stealing anything else. I'll have to go hungry. But where to hide?

All's quiet on the stairwell and I walk up, trying to look innocent, like I'm going to see a friend. At the top-floor landing, I step up to the roof access and try the door handle. It's locked. I return to the landing and look across through the windowless opening. Check the neighbouring roofs. Difficult to tell what kind of businesses are going on up there. I return to the street, walk three blocks, duck into another block of flats. Listen. I hear footsteps in the stairwell. Out I go again. Hopefully, the next block will be quiet. There I go: hoping. I need to concentrate. But I can't walk these streets much longer. I look up and I catch sight of clothes on a line, on a roof. A laundry? I slip into the building, climb the stairs, up to the roof access, and the steel door is open.

There's a man with his back to me, taking a sheet down from a line. I step onto the roof, sneak like a cat across to the far end of the roof and kneel down among the solar arrays. It's near perfect. With the clothes and sheets wafting, I'm well hidden. I couldn't have hidden like this on Ma Lexie's roof. It was too open. No, this is good.

———

The man returns to the roof every hour through the rest of the morning and afternoon, and not once does he lock the roof access door. It's a different setup to the one I knew before. No illegal workers. I guess, when he's carrying laundry, wet or dry, he doesn't want to mess with a lock. Anyway, there's nothing valuable up here.

I'm keeping an eye on the washing lines. I'd like to leave the roof with a warmer top for the night. I'll allow myself that, one more theft.

But when should I leave the roof? Too soon, and I'm exposed during daylight. Too late, and I risk getting locked on the roof at night. Because I can't rule that out as a possibility. He might lock the door when he takes down the last dry clothes.

Late afternoon, he reappears with another wet load. When he leaves the roof once again, I slip across to a rooftop standpipe, cup my hands, gulp down water and return to my hideout among the arrays. My hunger goes away with my stomach full of water. The streets below become noisier, children's voices too. I feel the urge to leave, but I know it's still too soon. But, jeez, if he locks up, I'll have to stay up here another day.

I find myself on my feet. Another bad decision? I cross the roof, stooping. I reach up and take a padded shirt off the line—I've had my eye on it for an hour at least. If I don't nab it now, the man will take it away. I fold it up and push it under my arm. I listen but my ears are ringing, just like my last moments on Ma Lexie's roof. I rush to the steel door, and, as I reach towards it, I hear footsteps on the stairs. I can't back off. The man pushes against the door with his palm, I barge past, knocking him hard against the wall, and I charge down the stairs. I reach the third floor before the man yells. I must have winded him. And I'm out on the street when I hear him shout from the roof. "Eh! Stop him!"

I dive down the first alley to the right, walking as fast as I dare, trying not to attract attention. Take the first street to the left, then the first alley to the right again. Zigzagging, slowing down to a steady walk. I shake out the shirt. It's patterned with green and brown leaves, but the inside is plain. I turn it inside out and pull it on over my first stolen shirt. A mother and child approach me, holding hands. The child jumps and skips while her mother takes long easy steps. Both smiling. They don't even glance at me.

Feels like six o'clock. Two hours until dusk, possibly. How to kill time? I'm tempted to lurk around the workshops on the edge of the enclave, position myself to make my run to the forest as soon as it's dark. But why take the risk of being spotted? Instead, I squeeze myself behind the rubbish bins at the final housing block. Not ideal. If anyone notices me here, what can I say? I won't be able to talk my way out of it. If I'm hiding, I must be in trouble.

After an hour, I'm cramping in my thighs. I shift to a kneeling position. I wish I had knee pads.

When it's as dark as it's likely to get here inside the enclave, and I'm daring myself to make a move, I hear someone humming a tune, and they're coming towards the bins. Whoever it is lifts the lid of the tall metal bin in front of me. The lid clanks closed. I don't know why, but I take it as a warning, a signal to go.

Javier was right. It's best to go it alone. And I'm not so lonely now. It's starting to feel quite normal. Truth is, I'm not completely alone. I wish I'd learned about birds at school, their songs. Why don't they teach you anything useful? The birds in England must be different from the ones back home, but I can guess the names of two or three that I hear in the forest. Like the woodpecker. I knew the name of this bird before I ever heard one in the wild—here. Wherever *here* is, some distance south of the River Mersey is all I know. I'm sure it's a woodpecker. I think it visits the dead oak tree by the clearing.

Everyone knows owls, but I swear no one hears as many as I do. Two families of owls live on opposite sides of this wooded valley. They call to one another, and their hooting can last an hour or more, but not every night. When they start their calling, I stop whatever I'm doing to listen. I can't help it—I remember Ma Lexie's dress, the pattern. I see her walking ahead of me on the roof.

The owls don't know I exist, or I don't think so. They don't care if I'm cold, if my tarp leaks in the night. But some of our problems are the same. They need to eat. They don't want any other owls invading their patch. The difference between the owls and me is this: I am on my own, while they stick together as a family. I'm pleased to share the night with them.

Mainly, I'm not too lonely because I'm busy. It's a full-time job living in the wild, and I'm getting to like it.

Last week, I moved my camp in a single day—a breakthrough for me after seven weeks in the forest. I'm better organised, and I need to be, with all the gear I've collected. I like to break camp every six or seven days, partly because I feel safer shifting around, and partly because the ground gets muddy if I stay too long in one place. That depends on the weather, how much it rains. At first, I picked bad sites and I had no choice but to move on. I learned that a dip in the ground might make me feel safe, better hidden, but it's the first place to fill with water. And when it rains here, it rains heavy. Nothing worse than waking up soaked to the skin. Also, when I pick a site, I look up into the trees. I could be crushed in my sleep if a strong wind rips off a dead branch.

My first break-ins were garden sheds. I found my tarp and a solar cooker, knives, ropes, a spade, containers for water, a bucket and an axe. It's surprising how many people keep tinned food in their sheds, like they've planned for the apocalypse. Now that I have the basics for living in the wild, I set out to rob houses with a mental shopping list. Helps me to focus, and to get in and out of properties as fast as I can. But I wish I could find a tent because that would help me stay in the woods until spring. By then, I'll feel safe to walk out of hiding. Though as time goes on, I like the idea of staying outdoors like this.

I broke into one house three weeks ago, the door left unlocked, and took a pile of winter clothing and a pair of hiking boots. Three bottles of whiskey too. My first taste of alcohol, real alcohol. I've had wine before, but never spirits. I take one slug of whiskey as I go to bed, enough to get me to sleep, and another when I wake up, to get myself going on these damp mornings. So, I've added spirits to every shopping list. I only wish I wasn't scared shitless when I go inside a stranger's house.

No one has seen me out here in the woods. Or if they have, they haven't bothered me. But I really pushed my luck one time, leaving the forest during a half-moon to climb an escarpment. I wanted to see the surrounding land. I stayed there until first light, and below me I saw a wide sweeping waterway. But, more exciting, I saw a straight line of water catching the orange rays of the sun. I felt a strong pull from that line of water. I felt tempted for a moment.

Today I plan to walk half an hour over difficult ground to a small group of houses that I've been watching during the past week. I've memorised the habits of the people living there: Who goes out to work and at what time. Who stays home most of the day. Who has visitors. How many deliveries are made and at what time they usually turn up. I haven't stolen anything from these houses yet. I hope the man who lives in the house nearest my route—the one I aim to hit today—leaves a window unlocked. If I can't get into the house, I'll take food from his vegetable plot and try next-door's house. If that fails, I'll open a couple of sheds. So, this is my eighth day, and this is the day I'll do my thieving, and tomorrow I'll move camp.

Two pairs of thick socks hang above my head in my shelter. It's a simple shelter: a tarp strung between two trees, and I've strung it low to keep it cosy. Warmer that way. I pull on both pairs of socks because the hiking boots I stole are a couple of sizes too big. Thieves can't be picky. They keep my feet dry, and that's the main thing. I shuffle forwards on my arse to the open side of the shelter—my head almost touching the tarp—grab my coat and check the pockets: torch, knife, gloves. I'll take the absolute essentials, nothing more, because I hope to be loaded up on my return. Pacing around the camp, I make my usual checks: one and a half containers of river water, a fair stock of bottled and tinned food. This camp is a good one, and I'd like to stay longer. It drains fast after rain. And a slight rise in the ground protects me from the colder north winds.

I open a bottle of sardines, eat half of them and lick the oil off my fingers. I don't eat much before a break-in. I've no appetite at all on days like this. Nervous as hell. But I need to eat before a tough walk.

I set out with my holdall and repeat my list, as if I'm talking to the trees. Little stuff that no one will notice is missing: soap, salt, chilli powder. Then the items that will be missed: spirits! And the outdoor stuff: windfall fruit, veggies from the gardens, tomatoes in the greenhouses. While I'm talking to the trees, I check my landmarks—the oak tree that's dead at the top, the mossy boulder, the embankment with the thin white trees, the stream below. I follow the stream, taking care when it passes close to one particular isolated house, where the owners are busy all the time—rushing in and out of the house, gardening, sweeping.

Reaching a point where the narrow valley widens out, I climb up the still-wooded slope and creep slowly towards the hamlet. With the roof of the nearest house in sight, I squat down and wait for the man who, at the same time every morning, leaves this house by its side door and walks his dog. He always takes a path below me, close to the edge of the stream. He'll return home after about twenty-five minutes and enter the house after scraping the mud off his boots. It doesn't give me much time, but he's reliable. I wonder what size boots he wears.

I've become a patient person. Though, in my gut, I hope the man won't appear. I hope he'll decide to stay home. Then I won't have to do this. I've been kidding myself lately that my thieving is a business. I have strategies and I'm definitely my own boss. But I feel a churning in my stomach, like I know my luck's about to run out.

Then I see him. Is he early today? The dog is off its lead already. Not normal. As soon as they reach the path he throws a ball for the dog. He hasn't done that before.

No big deal, I tell myself. But I don't like it. The man's changed his routine, not by much, but enough that I'm feeling sick. I wait and wait. I can't get to my feet. Truth is, I think I've lost my nerve. Five minutes or so later, I feel a few drops of rain. Big drops. Is that it? The man knew rain was coming? Sure enough, he's walking back down the path already. The rain's coming down heavy before the man reaches the side door of his house. He kicks the wall to get the worst of the mud off his boots and steps into his house without taking them off. And I'm getting wet as the rain drips down from the trees.

Seven, eight days of stalking, and nothing to show for it. I'll have to come back tomorrow. My stomach rumbles like never before.

I clamber over rocks as the valley narrows. It's the heaviest rain so far and a warning that life in the woods is going to get tougher. My hair is soaked and rain runs down my neck, soaking my clothes from the inside. There's a big old holly tree up ahead and it's a good place to shelter. But as I scramble towards it, I'm caught in a cloudburst. I can't see ahead. I'm drenched and as I pull myself over a large boulder, my hand slips. I fall back.

———

Been out cold for a while. I know that for sure because when I come around, the cloudburst has passed over, and I'm staring at the end of a rainbow. My head and eyes hurt, and I feel sharp pains when I try to move—in my ribs, in my back. I'm too scared to move again for several minutes. I don't want to know how much damage I've done. But I'm cold and wet. I roll onto my side, slowly shift my weight. I'm on hands and knees and push myself up to near standing. With a struggle, I climb over the wet rocks, picking a longer, easier route this time. The pain in my side is bad, but no worse than any knock from a rough tackle. I spot the holly tree. No point heading for that. It's more important to reach camp and get into dry clothes. It's slow going.

I'm miserable as hell when I kneel down by my tarp and start to strip off.

———

Sleep brings crazy dreams. I'm searching through drawers in my bedroom at home, looking for a football shirt, and everything I touch is soaked in blood. I'm awake, I think, and I'm sweating. My throat's raw. I can't find the water on my bedside table. That's when I know I'm still in a dream, and in this dream I'm desperate to pull off my clothes, but my arms won't move.

I know I'm awake when my fingers touch the soft tips of evergreen branches that make my bed. My head throbs. I'm cold, it's dark, but I don't know if the sun has just set, or if the sun might rise in an hour. I close my eyes again, not daring to move.

And then it's daylight. What part of the day, I've no idea. I crawl out from under the tarp and reach for the half-empty water container— it won't be so heavy. I swear, I'm as weak as a kitten, so thirsty. I take sips, can't control the flow, and water pours down my chin and onto my chest. I'm bare chested though I don't remember taking off my top. Sip by sip, I slowly fill my stomach with water, then spew it all out.

I abandon any thought of returning to the hamlet. I'm not well enough to move camp, so I lie down and crash asleep.

I spend three days feeling hot then cold, then hot again, telling myself I must try to drink water, that even if I vomit, any small amount of water I keep down will help. And I eat tinned pears. The sardine bottle also lies within reach. I dip my fingers into the sardine oil and suck them. Must be some goodness in that.

On the fourth day after my fall—or the fifth?—I feel strong enough to leave the shelter. I try to stand up, but I stoop forward, my hands grasping my knees. The camp is a mess from that first rainstorm. It has probably rained since. The tarp sags. The clothes I took off are soaked into the ground.

A thought drops on me like a rock falling from the sky, that if I had died here, animals would have found me before any other human. My face would be eaten off, and no one would know or care. I'd become a local horror story: the tramp eaten in the woods, maybe eaten alive. And if no one cares, what's the point? Since I came to England, has anyone given a damn about me?

I keep coming back to that moment in the market. She said sorry, said it wouldn't happen again. I didn't trust her, not then, but I never hated her. Honest, I believe she really liked me. And . . . am I crazy to see my business alongside hers—on the roof? Or has she totally forgotten me?

An idea creeps into my head, and I know I won't easily shake it off.

The sun peeps over the horizon, and I feel exposed on the escarpment. Yet it's a relief to leave the forest once again. I've walked for two days to reach this point, retracing my trek, stopping overnight at my previous camp. I took a wrong turn yesterday, missing one of my landmarks. Once I accepted I'd lost my way, I backtracked for over an hour and discovered my mistake. A large conifer branch had fallen on the landmark—now a crushed pile of rotten logs.

No clouds. A cold morning. I look down as the early light picks out the surface of the canal. Don't know which canal it is, but all the canals connect with one another, or so I've convinced myself. I've followed towpaths before, and I swear I can do it again if I stick to the rule: stay hidden until nightfall. From this high point, I plan a route down to the canal, then retrace my steps and retreat into dense forest, where I'll wait for nightfall.

With nothing to do, no camp to organise, no water to fetch, no thieving to plan, I have time to think, which might make another person lose their nerve. But not me. I take a blanket from my pack, wrap it around my shoulders and sit on a fallen tree. I'll save my energy because I'm still not fully fit. Closing my eyes, I feel that heart-bursting thing. You feel it when you sprint onto the football pitch as a late sub, knowing this is your moment. You know that you can, that you *will*, turn the game with your first touch. This feeling lifts me every time I take a big decision, when I know I'm about to change my life. Anything seems possible for a while. It's true. I believe in myself—and in new beginnings.

Apart from the big rule—stay hidden until nightfall—I remind myself of my other rules. It's okay to take a risk but make it a small one: Break into a shed instead of a house. Keep away from farm buildings because there's always a dog. If I see a good hideout halfway through the night, take it. It isn't a race. Last of all, expect the unexpected.

———

Not far down the towpath on that first night, the canal widened out. A channel led off to a giant steel structure. At first, I couldn't make sense of it. I felt as if I'd travelled back in time to another age. The canal junction, brightly lit, was a risky place to hang around, but when I spotted a visitor map I felt a massive wave of relief. I ran across and tried to take in all the information. The steel structure—the Anderton Boat Lift—linked the Trent and Mersey Canal, where I stood, with the River Weaver below. I traced the route of the Trent and Mersey with my finger, trying to memorise the route through Middlewich Locks, Wardle Canal and then the Shropshire Union.

With the route fixed in my head, I walk for the next five nights, finding hideouts in woods, in a derelict building, in a garden shed by

the canal side. One night I curled up at the side of a compost heap at
the bottom of a long garden.

I look at houses in a different way now. I believe I'll always live in
a flat, even when I'm rich. A flat that stretches across the entire floor of
a building. As big as six normal flats. Or I'll build my own house with
large gardens with no flower beds or sheds. I'll keep it simple. A big
square house, a lawn on all sides and a high perimeter fence.

I had one stroke of good fortune on my southerly journey. I broke
into a moored barge after watching it most of the day from my hideout.
No one came or went. The nearest barge was moored two hundred
metres away, and all seemed quiet there. At dusk, I smashed the lock
and let myself in. Scared shitless again. Flung open the cupboard doors.
Loads of dried and vacuum food. Filled my pack and pockets, and
legged it. Set up nicely, foodwise, I made good progress. The weather
was no worse than I expected. And, compared to my journey towards
Shropshire, I heard far fewer people and dogs on the towpaths while I
stayed hidden during the day.

But I was thrown, and I panicked like in a nightmare when I
couldn't find my journey's end. I thought I'd remember the long sweeping curve of the canal. I thought I'd recognise the spot of woodland
with a canal embankment and a steep slope up to the fields. Expect the
unexpected. But I imagined the unexpected as, I don't know, someone
jumping out on me, or breaking my arm in a fall, or an early snowfall. I
was tired, too, and I started taking risks, walking at first light, forwards
and backwards along the canal, hoping to find the right place. Total
failure. So, I decided I hadn't walked far enough and pushed on three
or four miles along the towpath. I came to a curve in the canal that felt
right. At long last, I found the woods where Odette and I had stopped
on that first night.

———

Six nights it's taken me now to pick out a route through the fields. Odette hadn't talked much that night we escaped, but she did say that if we headed south from the enclave, we were bound to find a canal. I told her we needed to keep the North Star behind us. But, retracing our escape hasn't been simple. I can't walk directly towards the North Star because the fields are strange shapes, and I'm forced to go off course to find field gates and stiles.

I think it's Friday today. And I've no choice. I must enter the enclave tomorrow because I'm down to eating rotten apples, the last windfalls of the year. I wait until dark, wash myself as best I can in murky canal water, and set out.

It's about four in the morning when I reach the last field. I huddle down in the hedgerow. A quiet country road separates me from the open ground bordering the southern end of the enclave. I scrape mud off my boots with my knife. I drink the last of my water. I take a piss.

What have I got to lose? In my head I shout *Fuck all* as I climb over the field gate and hurry across to the low-rise buildings. I find a workshop that's padlocked, windows thick with dirt, and squeeze myself into a doorway set back from the line of the building. Can't do much else. If I hear anyone approach, I'll move on.

And so, when I hear the first sounds from the housing blocks— shutters being opened—I dump my pack and filthy coat and head towards the market, hoping I look like a local lad heading home after an all-nighter. Honest to God, I stink. No mistake about that. Damp clothes and sweat.

———

It isn't Saturday. It's Sunday.

Stallholders in the vegetable market are still loading farm produce onto tables. Kids on ladders, tying up and stretching canopies. Fewer tables than I expected. That's how I know what day it is—it's a later start on a Sunday, with half the number of stalls. Without thinking I veer to get a better look at a girl with dark hair who's adding parsnips to an already-big pile. An older woman gives her a nudge and nods towards me, smirking. Can they smell me? They must be disgusted. I lurch away and feel my face and ears burning. The first girl I see, and I act like an idiot. I blink like crazy.

I pace through Clothing Street, but I can't keep a straight line. I feel drunk. So much noise, all these people. And it's not even busy yet. Every second pitch is still empty. I try to remember the market from a single day, four years ago, when I helped Ma Lexie on the stall. That day should have been special—the start of something good.

Will the same businesses be here? Will the stalls be set out on the same pitches as they were years ago? I stumble. A woman reaches towards me but has second thoughts, backs off.

I reach the far end of the street as the pink sheet is hoisted up by two lads my own age.

I'm too early. I take a right at the end of Clothing Street and pretend I'm interested in a second-hand bookstall. It's not a stall though. The books stand on a waist-high wall, with the book spines facing the sky. The bookseller is still arranging them. He notices me after a couple of minutes and calls across, "Fiction, that end. Nonfiction, this end." I choke up and dip my head. It's the first time someone has spoken to me since I left the indenture camp. My body's shaking, like microshaking, and it takes courage to speak, to check my voice still works. "Any books about birds, wildlife?"

"One, somewhere. I haven't unpacked it yet."

"I'll come back."

"Okay, mate. I'll keep it to one side."

I stick around, touching the books without reading the titles, feeling relieved that I pass as a normal punter.

———

As if a bell has rung for the opening of the market, the streets become overrun by early shoppers—in a couple of minutes. It's safer, so I join the flow and stroll back down Clothing Street, passing one jumble stall after another. I have no clear memories of the street. Was it like this before? I remind myself that Ma Lexie might be going through bad times, like me, might be dealing in jumble herself. She might have moved on, left the enclave.

I'm distracted by two teenagers. Their arms around one another, laughing and joshing. Makes me angry. All my years locked away. I hate how happy they are. I barge past them. But I stop dead.

I see her. No mistake. Ma Lexie, just as I remember her.

The teenagers push past me.

I'm not ready. I cross the street and stand behind a stall selling bags, press myself against a wall. My legs are ready to buckle. Ma Lexie is only twenty or so metres away, and I realise I haven't imagined this part, what to say.

She unpacks a garment box, places the empty box in a trolley, which she pushes to the back of her pitch. It's a new trolley—bigger, with four wheels. And the stall is wider than I remember. A double stall? My heart is pounding. I've found her. She's doing well, or I think so, which means she's in a good mood. How the hell will she react? Badly?

Another stallholder calls across to Ma Lexie, and her face breaks into a smile, ear to ear. I hear Ma Lexie laughing.

My feet put roots into the ground. Still too soon.

Her hair is longer.

Before she has even finished hanging garments around her stall, she chats with a customer and makes a sale. I smile to myself, for I remember she always gave a discount on her first sale of the day, to bring good luck. She's happy. The signs look good. I walk closer and stand directly opposite her stall, staring at her. The street is busy with shoppers, and I lean from side to side to keep her in my line of sight.

I pull my ragged hair away from my face, and in that moment she looks up. I think she catches a glimpse of me. Maybe not. I wait. With the next gap in the stream of shoppers, I see she's staring straight at me. Neither of us moves. Shoppers cut across.

I can't rush. She needs time to think.

She places her left palm flat against her forehead. Looking straight at me, she smiles and frowns at the same time.

That's my cue. I walk towards her.

ACKNOWLEDGMENTS

I take immense pleasure in thanking Robert, Adam and Garry Charnock, always my first readers, for their insightful comments on my manuscript. I am also particularly grateful to Nina Allan and Christopher Priest for a valuable discussion during the early stages of this writing project. Similarly, I've enjoyed a number of helpful conversations with Matthew De Abaitua, Fiona Curran, Matt Hill, Helen Marshall and E. J. Swift. Additional thanks are due to Nina and Matt for their comments on my completed manuscript. I have also enjoyed the support of NewCon Press, publisher of my novella, *The Enclave*, on which the opening chapters of this novel are based.

Working with my editor, Jason Kirk, is always a great pleasure, and I am grateful not only to Jason but also to the whole 47North team. My thanks, too, go to my wonderful agent, Sarah Such.

ABOUT THE AUTHOR

Photo © 2018 Marzena Pogorzaly

Anne Charnock is the author of *Dreams Before the Start of Time*, winner of the 2018 Arthur C. Clarke Award. Her debut novel, *A Calculated Life*, was a finalist for the 2013 Philip K. Dick Award and the 2013 Kitschies Golden Tentacle Award. The *Guardian* featured *Sleeping Embers of an Ordinary Mind* in "Best Science Fiction and Fantasy Books of 2015." Anne's novella, *The Enclave*, won the 2017 British Science Fiction Association Award for Short Fiction. Her writing career began in journalism, and her articles appeared in the *Guardian, New Scientist, International Herald Tribune,* and *Geographical.* Learn more at www.annecharnock.com.